4/95

D1014977

SHADOWMAKER

Joan Lowery Nixon

SHADOWMAKER

Delacorte Press

Published by
Delacorte Press
Bantam Doubleday Dell Publishing Group, Inc.
1540 Broadway
New York, New York 10036

Library of Congress Cataloging in Publication Data

Nixon, Joan Lowery.
    Shadowmaker / by Joan Lowery Nixon.
        p.   cm.
    Summary: Soon after she and her mother come to the small Texas town
of Kluney and experience a series of menacing events, Katie begins to
suspect that there is something sinister going on.
    ISBN 0-385-32030-2
    [1. Crime—Fiction. 2. City and town life—Texas—Fiction. 3. Texas
—Fiction.] I. Title. II. Title: Shadowmaker.
PZ7.N65Sk   1994
[Fic]—dc20   93-32314   CIP   AC

Manufactured in the United States of America

Designed by Joseph Rutt

May 1994

10 9 8 7 6 5 4 3 2 1

BVG

With love to Hershell Nixon,
the number one inspiration in my life

SHADOWMAKER

CHAPTER ONE

I woke when the German shepherd barked, his sharp warning slicing through my dream. Without street-lights or moonlight my room was so dark I was disori-ented, and I fought to kick off the sheet that was tangled around my legs.

This wasn't our apartment in Houston. Where was I?

As I struggled from sleep I recognized the excited bay of the yellow Labrador far down the road and the snarling slathering of the rottweiler on the nearby Emery place. As my head cleared I remembered that I was in the old beach house that Mom and I had moved to a few days before. I knew, from just my limited experience with that row of hyper, fenced-in dogs, that not only had someone just walked down the road that dead-ended at our house, but whoever had come this way was still out there. We didn't

1

have a dog, but we didn't need one. Those three were watchdogs for everyone on the road.

The illuminated numbers on my bedside clock glowed one-twenty. No one had any reason to be on our road at that time of night. Quietly, I moved inch by inch toward the glass French doors that overlooked the north side of the house, trying not to stub my toes on the books and shoes and other things I'd scattered across the floor. Before I'd climbed into bed I opened one of the doors a few inches so I could enjoy the sound of the wavelets that slapped the shore and the salty-sour dampness of the night air, but now I felt an urgent need to close and lock the door.

Just as my fingertips touched the cool metal knob, a voice whispered in my ear, "Katie! Hurry!"

I jumped and squealed at the same time, and the door banged shut.

Mom reached across to turn the key in the lock. "Don't make so much noise," she cautioned. "Someone's out there."

We pressed our faces against the glass, trying to peer through the blackness, but the pale light from the thin slice of new moon was too faint to penetrate the shadows. The dogs, having given their warnings, began to lose interest, but they kept up an insistent barking, as though they weren't sure when they were supposed to stop.

My heart jumped, and I grabbed Mom's shoulder as near the road a dark shadow shifted. "Something just moved over by the gate," I whispered. "See . . . under that twisted oak tree? I think there's a person standing there."

The muscles in Mom's shoulder tensed. "Yes. And over

there . . . next to the garage . . . There's more than one of them."

"More than one of *who?*" I asked. "Who's out there and why are they here in the middle of the night? What are they doing?"

Mom suddenly reached up and pulled the heavy cotton drapes across the glass doors. She flipped on my bedroom light and picked up the phone on the table next to my bed. "That's for the sheriff to find out," she said, and jabbed at the buttons on the phone.

The dogs suddenly went into action again—this time with the rottweiler working himself into a frenzy, the shepherd joining in, and the Lab in the distance picking up the pace. The shadowmakers who'd been outside our house were heading away.

"The sheriff will be here in about fifteen minutes," Mom told me as she hung up the phone. "I'm going to make some coffee. Do you want a cup?"

"Sure," I said, and reached for my T-shirt and jeans, but Mom stopped me by wrapping me in a quick hug.

"I thought Kluney would be safe and quiet. I'm sorry, Katie," she said apologetically.

"Why are you apologizing?" I tried to keep resentment from my voice. I hadn't wanted to come to Kluney in the first place, but I didn't have a choice. "We don't know who was out there or why. What makes you think they'd have something to do with you?"

"The letters . . ." she began, and let her words drift into silence.

I knew what letters she meant—insulting, ugly things,

some even with veiled threats, all of them anonymous, of course. It wasn't the first time Mom had received angry letters after one of her newspaper exposés had been published.

After a record number of Brownsville babies had been born with serious birth defects, Mom had questioned the activities of the factories in the Brownsville area. Had toxic wastes been dumped into the water that fed the resacas? Or had pesticides used on the large farms upstream seeped their poisons into the water? She'd been accused of fabricating charges in an attack against big business.

Mom demanded answers and urged the local people to demand a government study. The residents were promised the study, but were told that it would take at least two years in order for it to be accurate. Mom is, was, and always will be a crusader. She couldn't ignore the plight of those babies born without brain stems, and their heartbroken parents, and she also couldn't ignore the suspected toxic contamination that might have caused it. She *had* to make it public through her national column.

"You've told me yourself that most people who write angry, mean letters never follow through," I said. "And if they really wanted to hurt us, wouldn't they think of something better to do to us than hide by our fence and stare at the house?"

"You're right, Katie," Mom answered, and tried a smile that was more wobbly than reassuring. "Better get dressed. The sheriff should be here soon."

As I pulled on my jeans and a T-shirt, then sat waiting

for the coffee to finish dripping into the glass pot, I thought about Mom's work and her achievements.

A few years ago a man was sentenced to death in Huntsville, but he maintained he was innocent. Mom believed him when he said evidence in the case was first withheld, then "lost." Mom covered the situation, and her columns—added to other newspaper stories and television coverage—helped people get angry enough that legal steps were taken. The man was freed, and rightly so.

Then there was a businessman who tried to murder his wife and incriminated someone else. Mom's columns helped bring about the just outcome in that situation too. National and regional magazines feature her articles, and because of the investigative coverage, lots of people know her byline. She hasn't won a Pulitzer prize yet, but Mom never stops until she gets the story.

As she put a cup of steaming coffee and a small pitcher of milk in front of me, we heard a car pull up in front of our gate. Heavy footsteps thumped across the cement walk that led past the French doors in my bedroom around to the kitchen door.

This house, which Mom inherited from her uncle Jim, is a compact, one-story wooden structure without a real front door. The front room and the covered porch beyond it overlook a broad stretch of dunes and sea grass rolling down to the sea, so everyone who comes to the house has to enter through the kitchen.

That didn't seem to bother the sheriff. He was a large, paunchy, beef-red man who more than filled out his uniform. "Everett J. Granger," he growled, after Mom intro-

5

duced us to him. He shook her hand. "I remember you from when you used to come to see your uncle. Last time you were in town was at his funeral."

Mom pulled out one of the rickety wooden kitchen chairs for him, and I winced as he lowered his stocky frame into it. The chair shuddered, but it held tight.

He took a sip of the hot coffee, then looked around the kitchen before he spoke. "It's been a while since I was sittin' here with your uncle Jim. This house stood vacant so long, I wondered if Jim's kin would ever come around to make use of it."

Mom nodded. There was no reason she had to explain why we were here, but Sheriff Granger didn't see it that way. "So how come, after all these years, you show up now?" he asked.

Not many people get Mom flustered, but the sheriff managed to do so, maybe because in this case Mom wasn't too sure of herself.

"You make it sound like such a long time," she said. She stirred her coffee vigorously, then dropped her spoon with a clatter. "My uncle died only four years ago."

"And . . . ?" One of Sheriff Granger's eyebrows was poised higher than the other, like a bushy question mark. He waited for Mom's answer.

She took a deep breath and straightened her shoulders. "I'm a writer," she said. "I write a syndicated newspaper column."

His eyebrow came down and he said, "That's common knowledge. So's the fact that you're used to pokin' around courthouses, pryin' into private records, and makin' people mad."

Mom was caught by surprise. "The investigations I do are perfectly legal!"

The sheriff looked unconvinced. "Legal or not, let's get one thing straight. I hope you're not fixin' to do any of your investigations around Kluney. A number of folks have been wonderin' just what it is you're lookin' for. Whatever it is, they don't like it."

Mom actually blushed. "I'm here to write a novel."

He took a long swig of coffee, then asked, "Yeah? What kind of a novel does a reporter write?"

His question came out like a challenge, and after a moment's confusion Mom reacted defensively. "What kind? Mainstream, not nonfiction investigative reporting. You do understand the difference?"

I winced, but the sheriff just turned to Mom and said, "As Francis Bacon wrote, 'Some books are to be tasted, others to be swallowed, and some few to be chewed and digested.' "

Mom's mouth opened, but nothing came out. *Bacon, Francis Bacon,* I thought. *Wasn't he some British writer back in the early sixteen hundreds?*

"A smart lady like you must have read Francis Bacon, haven't you?" Sheriff Granger asked.

"Touché," Mom replied. "I just wasn't expecting you to quote someone like Francis Bacon."

"Because I'm a sheriff? Or because I'm small-town?" He shifted a bit and his chair wobbled. "I helped organize the local Classical Reading Society in Kluney."

7

Mom's cheeks flushed even pinker, so I interrupted. "Aren't you supposed to be questioning us about why we called you?" I asked.

"I'll be gettin' around to that," he said. "Your mama invited me to a cup of coffee first, and there's no need not to be sociable." His glance at me intensified, and he asked, "You registered in our high school, Katherine?"

"Yes."

"Sophomore? Junior?"

"Sophomore."

He nodded, satisfied. "It's hard to come to a new school in the middle of the spring semester. Makin' friends?"

"Sure." I suddenly became interested in the bottom of my coffee cup. I wondered if he could possibly know that what I'd told him was a lie. It had taken a couple of days to scrub down this house before we could move into it, so I'd only been at Kluney High on Thursday and Friday. During those two days I'd been looked over and talked about—the kids made that obvious—but only a couple of them had said so much as *hello* to me. Lana Jean Willis, a skinny girl with bad skin and dirty blond hair, was the only one who'd tried to be friendly.

"You sure favor your mama with that red hair and blue eyes," Sheriff Granger told me. "I don't know of any other redheads in these parts, except for Sally, who's a waitress in Denny's over on the highway, but Sally was a blonde before she became a redhead, so I don't guess we can count her."

The sheriff bent back his head, draining the coffee from his cup. "Let's get down to business," he said, and pulled out a notebook and pencil. Turning each page by licking his thumb, he finally found an empty page and began to write. "Eve Gillian," he said to Mom. "Two *l*'s in Gillian?"

"That's right," Mom answered. "Now, what happened was—"

"Hold on," he said. "I'm writin' down your address. Give me your telephone number too."

Finally, he raised his head and said, "Okay. Now, according to Doris, our dispatcher, some folks were on the road out beyond your place around one-fifteen this mornin', and after a few minutes they left."

"There's more to it than that!" Mom's eyes flashed.

"Like what? Did they come onto your property?"

"No. At least, I don't think so. They were at the gate and next to the garage."

"Any threats? Did they call out? Use obscenities or anything like that?"

"No! They were just . . . just *there*."

"You told Doris you'd been asleep. How did you know anybody was there?"

"Because of the dogs in those yards that back onto the road. They woke us with their barking."

The sheriff smiled. "Yeah. I can see how those three dogs would wake anybody, livin' or dead, exceptin' their owners." He studied his notebook for a moment, then asked, "Were any of the folk you saw out there armed?"

"I don't know. It was too dark to tell."

"Too dark? But you said you saw them."

Mom couldn't take any more. She rested her elbows on the table and leaned forward, her forehead in the palms of her hands.

I stepped in again. "Their shadows moved. That's how we knew there was more than one person."

"Okay," Sheriff Granger said, and wrote something. "How many people were out there?"

"Uh . . . at least two."

"Just two?"

"There might have been more."

"Male or female?"

"We don't know."

"But they didn't do anything or say anything?"

"They frightened us."

"How?"

Mom dropped her arms and slapped the table in exasperation. "By just being there!"

Sheriff Granger slowly and deliberately closed his notebook and tucked it away with his pencil. "Miz Gillian," he said, "that's a public road. Far as I can see, no one did anything except walk down that road."

"But the road ends at our gate! No one would have any reason for being there unless they had business with us."

"Coulda been folks out for a stroll, maybe a young couple lookin' for a quiet place. There's nothin' to show us it was anythin' more threatenin' than that." His lips turned up in a bare suggestion of a smile. "Remember what Sir James Matthew Barrie said? 'A house is never still in darkness to those who listen intently. . . . Ghosts were created when the first man woke in the night.' "

"The Little Minister," Mom mumbled, and I almost expected her to add "show off," but instead she said, "I didn't call you about a ghost. I called about prowlers."

His smile stretched to its full width. "I've heard that folks in Houston see so much crime they're always thinkin' they'll be next. Well, you don't have to worry here in Kluney."

"You're kidding, aren't you?" I blurted out. "Crimes take place everywhere, even in small towns."

"Oh, we got crime, of sorts," he said, and rubbed his chin. "In fact, lately we've had a little more than usual. To my way of thinkin', the amount of crime depends on who's stoppin' off or movin' through town."

"Your own citizens are squeaky-clean?" Mom asked.

Sheriff Granger went on as though he hadn't heard the disbelief in Mom's voice. "We keep tabs on our own."

I was too curious to let the subject drop. "What kind of crimes do you get?" I asked.

He shifted his weight, and the chair trembled. I was really getting worried about the fate of that chair. "Shop-liftin' . . . burglaries," he answered. "Earlier this year we had a string of shopliftin' reports. Started out with some minor stuff, like pocketknives and flashlights, hardly worth botherin' about; but then stuff like VCRs, camcorders, and such got taken. A motorcycle gang came through town around that time, and there were a couple of other people from out of town we all had our doubts about."

"You didn't catch the shoplifters?"

His forehead puckered and grew a little redder. "My jurisdiction extends only so far. I can't go huntin' down folks who are long gone afore I get the shopliftin' reports."

He shifted toward Mom, but I wanted to know the rest. "You said *burglaries* too. What about them?"

11

"Yeah . . . Funny thing about 'em, they started around the time the shopliftin' stopped and, like the shopliftin', they didn't amount to much at first—a few small office supplies, some auto tools, a case of beer. Then some folks got their homes broken into."

Mom looked interested in spite of herself. "Maybe that's what was planned for us tonight."

"I doubt it," the sheriff said. "Burglars don't want to be seen or heard. It'd be too hard to burglarize a small house like this while people are in it."

"Hasn't anybody been able to identify the burglars?" I asked.

Sheriff Granger shook his head. "You're thinkin' of robbery, which is a more serious crime than burglary. Folks tend to get the two mixed up. Robbers are the ones who hold you up with a gun. Burglars come around when you're gone or when you're asleep and take what they want and get away fast. Usually, nobody sees burglars."

A sudden thought seemed to come to the sheriff. His eyes darkened and deepened, drilling into Mom's eyes, and I realized he wasn't always the easygoing man he seemed to be. "Let's get back to your reason for calling me. Is there anything you haven't mentioned, Miz Gillian? Like maybe a husband somewhere tryin' to give you a bad time?"

Mom closed her eyes, as though she wanted to shut out both the sheriff and unhappy memories. "My husband died in a car accident six years ago," she answered.

"Sorry," he murmured, and his voice softened. "Then let me try a different direction. Anybody tryin' to repossess your car? Anybody you're havin' trouble with?"

I waited for Mom to bring up the Brownsville articles, but I remembered what the sheriff had said about Mom making people upset with her columns. She must have remembered too. She jutted her chin out stubbornly and answered, "No. Nothing like that."

"Then we're through here," Sheriff Granger said. "I'll be goin'. If anythin' else worries you, just give me a call. That's what I'm here for."

Without answering, Mom led him to the door. The moment he was outside she locked it firmly, then turned and leaned against it.

"It's weird," I said. "Sheriff Granger actually looks like he's playing the part of a small-town sheriff on TV. I couldn't believe it when he started to quote passages from great literature. Mom, it doesn't add up."

"It does seem odd, but as a journalist I've learned never to assume I know what a person is going to be like. You're trying to make him fit into a category," Mom said. "We're all guilty at times of categorizing people, even though we know better."

"But the sheriff has a stomach that laps over his belt, he drops his *g*'s, and he calls you Miz. Is he for real?"

"Why can't he have a good mind and a love of good literature?" Mom asked.

"It's still kind of weird," I mumbled, unwilling to give up easily, "and even if you won't say it, I know you agree."

"Tomorrow," Mom said in a low voice, as she took another look at the door, "I'll get some dead bolts and window locks at the hardware store, and a couple of bright lights I can string up in the backyard. Those French doors

. . . I don't like all that glass. Maybe at the store they can suggest something that will help me secure them."

"Mom?" I asked, shuddering from the chill that ran up my backbone into my neck. "You think whoever was out there will come back, don't you? But it's not connected to Brownsville and the articles, is it?"

She looked surprised for a moment, and I had the strange feeling that she'd forgotten I was there. "Oh, Katie," she said, and strode across the room to clasp my shoulders, hugging me tightly. "Don't mind my ramblings. I was just talking to myself, just taking extra precautions. I didn't mean to frighten you, baby. I don't know what to think, but I know that we need to be careful."

I wanted to reassure her that I was all right and no longer a baby to be worried about, but when I opened my mouth a huge, noisy yawn came out.

Mom smiled. "We're both exhausted. Let's forget all about this craziness and get to bed. Okay?"

"Okay," I answered, and walked off toward my room at the back of the house. I held the curtains back so I could stare out the window into the darkness, searching for movement among the shadows, yet terrified that I might see it. I wished Mom had answered my questions. It wasn't okay.

CHAPTER TWO

It was misery waking to the alarm clock, and the chill of the bare wood floor stung my toes. At least the floors were clean—scrubbed and waxed and polished until Mom was satisfied—a huge improvement on the way they'd looked when we'd first arrived at the house and stepped inside.

The badly worn boards had been gritty with beach sand and dirt and scuffed with a mixture of bare footprints and the intricate design of whirls and whorls from the imprints of sports shoes. Crushed beer and soft drink cans lay in the mess, and a couple of ashtrays filled with butts decorated the tables.

"I thought we'd find something like this when I discovered the door was unlocked," Mom had said, making a face at the room. "It looks like a few beach bums found a free place to flop for the night."

I immediately looked over my shoulder, and Mom smiled. "Katie, honey," she said, "they're long gone. Look at the dust on that table."

It didn't look any different to me than the dust lying everywhere. What an awful place to have to live! "Maybe we could get a hose and just wash everything down," I suggested.

"Better yet," Mom said, "help me move the furniture out on the porch. Then fill that bucket over there with water and soap, and let's get to work. This little house is going to look one hundred percent better when we're through cleaning it."

I didn't believe it, but Mom was right. We scrubbed everything, including the walls, threw out the drapes and curtains, and hung new ones Mom had bought for the bedrooms and bathroom. The other windows she left open to the sea.

"What about the attic?" As I stood in the short hallway that joined the two bedrooms with a bath between them, I glanced upward at the rectangle in the ceiling with a short rope dangling from it. I knew that meant folding stairs. "Do we have to clean the attic too?"

"No. We've reached the end of our cleaning, thank goodness," Mom said as she flopped into the nearest kitchen chair. "Uncle Jim wasn't interested in possessions. He owned very little, and what he didn't need he gave away. He told me once he only went into the attic when roof repairs were needed, so we won't find anything up there except more dust."

"And maybe mouse droppings and rapid bats," I'd added.

Mom laughed and threw her cleaning rag at me. "Let's wash up," she said, "and cook our first meal in our new house."

Mom may have been eager to live there, but I wasn't. For one thing, no matter what we did to it, the house still looked ancient and tired and dried-out, like dead leaves or old paper. It wasn't anything like our big apartment in Houston.

And for another thing, I missed the High School for the Performing Arts and my specialty field of dance so much it was like an ache that wouldn't go away. "You've got what it takes, Katie," the ballet instructor had told me, even though he understood that ballet was not my career goal but just my private love. No matter how high he'd set my goals, I worked with all my strength to meet them.

Maybe it sounds weird that I never told anyone—even Mom—how much I loved ballet. Each time I practiced, each time I performed, the steps would become part of the music. The music would blend with my mind, and my body would follow with a joy that could have shone clear and golden, if anyone else could have seen it. But they didn't, because I hugged my feelings to myself. Maybe I shouldn't have.

One day Mom sat with me, her eyes glittering with excitement, and explained that she wanted to take six months leave from her column and magazine writing and write a novel. She explained that while she was writing the novel there would be very little money coming in, and staying in Uncle Jim's old beach house, on which she'd kept up the tax payments, would save our biggest expense —monthly rent.

My words came out in a ragged croak. "But my dance lessons? The school musical?" My voice broke, and I couldn't finish.

"You're talented in so many directions, Katie—dance too —and I know you enjoy your ballet lessons," Mom said.

The words zinged inside my head like a tennis ball gone crazy. *Enjoy my lessons? Enjoy? Couldn't Mom understand that my love of dance was so much more than "enjoy"?*

No. Of course she couldn't, and it was my fault, because my love of ballet was too private to share.

I guessed that Mom was trying to read my face, because she looked sort of puzzled, then sad and vulnerable as she told me the plan for letting our apartment go and storing the furniture. "We won't do it unless you agree, Katie," she said. "I know it's hard for you, or anybody else, to understand, but this story I want to write has been taking over my mind. Mentally, I'm inventing whole chunks of dialogue, and visualizing scenes, and living more with my imaginary characters than with the real people around me. The story has to come out. I *have* to write it."

Strangely enough, I did understand. Even though I was sure I'd never want to be a published writer, like Mom, I realized what she was trying to tell me. I keep a journal, and sometimes I just have to write down my thoughts and feelings. It's like an itch that starts in my brain and drives me crazy. I can't ignore it.

Mrs. Gantner taught us to keep journals when I was in eighth grade, and I'll always be grateful that she did. She'd look through our journals, to make sure we were on the right track, but whatever we wrote was private, and she never talked about content, even to us. Once, I wrote my thoughts about ballet in a kind of poetry that pulled the music from my body and laid it out on the paper in the form of words. Mrs. Gantner told me my poem was good and she was glad I liked to experiment with word forms, so since then I wrote a lot of poetry in my journal. Maybe it was good, maybe not, but it doesn't matter. Nobody had ever seen it except me.

Mrs. Walgren, my English lit teacher at Kluney High, was also big on journals. She seemed pleased when I told her I'd been keeping one. I guess she didn't want to have to explain all over again how to do it to the new student. She had asked us to turn in our journals over the weekend, so I brought mine Friday and added it to the stack.

I was eager to get it back because I wanted to write about what had happened last night. It's easy for me to sort out ideas, feelings, problems, and all that stuff by putting them into words on paper.

I gobbled down a quick breakfast, grabbed my books, and walked along our road about three blocks to where it intersects with the main road into town. The dogs knew me pretty well by now, but they came running down the long slope from their houses, which were almost out of sight on the next road north, and leaped against their chain-link fences, showing me, with a few halfhearted barks, that they were on constant duty.

I took a few moments to talk to each dog, so I had to run the last few feet to catch the school bus.

The bus was loaded with junior high boys—all loud mouths and big feet. I squirmed through them to the nearest empty seat and plopped down, out of balance as the bus took off. This was pickup truck country, and I doubted if there were more than two dozen kids in the entire high school who didn't drive pickups to school.

One of the have-nots was sitting near me—a small, quiet, brown-haired girl who was in most of my classes. I remembered her name—Tammy Ludd.

"Hi," she said.

"Hi," I answered, and opened my history book. Lana Jean had told me that Mrs. DeJohn, in history, liked to give pop quizzes on Mondays, and I wanted to look over the chapter I'd read Friday night.

"Did you have any trouble with that chart we had to make for biology?" Tammy asked.

"No. It took a lot of time, that's all," I said, and tried to read.

There was silence for a moment, but Tammy spoke again, and I could hear an edge of anger in her voice. "Why do city people think they're better than us?"

I looked up, surprised. "They don't."

"*You* do. Look at you—reading a book so you won't have to talk to me."

"That's not why I was reading. If we're going to have a test . . ." I closed the book and tucked it in with my other books. "I'm sorry. I guess I did seem rude. It's just that . . . I didn't think anyone at Kluney High cared if I talked to them or not."

A brief smile flickered over Tammy's lips, and she said, "I've gone to school with the same kids since kindergarten. Some of them are nice. Some aren't. But even some of the nice ones kind of stick to who they know. It's not just that you're from the city. It's more that because your mother's a famous reporter your life's probably pretty exciting and nothing like you'd find down here."

"So you're all going to snub me before I get a chance to snub you?"

She stared at me for a minute before she answered. "I guess it must seem that way, but that's not how it's meant."

"Let me put things straight," I said. "My mom has saved up enough money to get us through the next six months, if no emergency comes up. We're living in the house her uncle left her because living there is cheap. Mom's here to write a novel, and when she finishes we'll go back to Houston, and I'll go back to the High School for the Performing Arts." I paused, then added, "And, for what it's worth, our life in Houston isn't that exciting."

"What's the High School for the Performing Arts?" Tammy asked.

"A regular high school, only the students spend extra time working in dance or drama or music or photography —one of the arts."

"Neat," she said, and looked at me with curiosity. "Which were you?"

"Dance—ballet."

Tammy grinned. "Julie was right. She said you walk like the ballet dancers she saw in Houston."

I grinned right back. "Like a duck, with toes pointed out." And when Tammy began to remonstrate, I said, "It's the way we stretch our muscles."

"Don't you have to keep up your lessons?" Tammy suddenly asked. "I mean, there's nobody around here who teaches ballet."

"I know," I said, and turned toward the window, blinking hard. All I could do was keep up my practice sessions, but that was hard in our little house without room for anything much beyond the basic positions and with only the top of the chest of drawers in my bedroom to serve as the barre.

As the bus bumped and rocked over the curb next to the drive leading to the schools' joint parking lot, Tammy said, "We have lunch the same period. If you want, come on over to our table."

"Thanks," I said, and winced as the junior high boys, yelling and shouting, shoved and pushed, trying to be first to get off the bus.

English lit was first period, and I bumped into Lana Jean outside the classroom door. I noticed her fingernails weren't clean and there was something that looked like a grease stain on her sweater. "I'm scared," she said.

"Scared? Of what?" I asked. I thought of myself and my mother last night.

She hunched her shoulders as she gave a long sigh. "Of getting our journals back. Mrs. Walgren keeps giving me awful grades and telling me I don't understand what journal writing is all about. But I *have* to pass English lit. My mom will kill me if I don't."

I sighed. I was never really scared of getting a bad grade. I couldn't imagine how anyone could flunk keeping a journal. "It's going to be okay," I said and opened the door to the classroom. A huge guy named Billy Don Knipp twisted in his seat by the window and smiled at me. He had a gap in his teeth where one had probably been knocked out. I was not the least impressed, but I smiled back, still feeling good about Tammy's invitation.

Mrs. Walgren, round and pink with a halo of gray hair, beamed at me with enthusiasm, which puzzled me. I didn't have time to find out what was making her so happy, because the bell jangled in our ears and we dropped into our seats.

We tried to look like we were paying attention through the long list of office intercom announcements and the beginning-of-the-week quote of inspiring thoughts—this time from the Spanish Club. Finally, with a squawk the intercom was silenced, and Mrs. Walgren got to her feet.

"I'm going to return your journals to you," she said. "Most of you are doing well—I've made just a few comments here and there—and I want you to continue writing in these journals daily until the end of the semester."

There were a few groans, and a couple of guys put their heads down on their arms.

"Could I sharpen my pencil?" a girl in the back row asked.

"Not now," Mrs. Walgren said. "As usual, I'll read a few of the best entries to inspire the rest of you."

I sat up straight, cold needles darting up and down my spine. She couldn't do that, could she? What about privacy? Mrs. Gantner gave us privacy. I took it for granted that all teachers would teach journal writing the same way. For just an instant I closed my eyes as I realized what I had written.

Don't panic! I told myself. *You're a new student. She isn't likely to read from your journal.* But I remembered that brilliant smile she gave me and understood what it had meant. I wished I could slide under my desk and disappear forever.

We heard Billy Don Knipp's description of the last ten minutes of a football game, and I discovered that Billy Don, the big guy with the embarrassed look on his face, played halfback for Kluney High.

"Although your journals are basically supposed to deal with your current thoughts and feelings, it's perfectly all right to relive an earlier experience and write about it," Mrs. Walgren said when she'd finished reading Billy Don's journal entry. "Sometimes the experience becomes even more definitive over the passage of a few months." She smiled as she handed Billy Don's journal back. "I remember that game. November sixth, a home game against Crossview High, and we won, twenty-one to seven."

The journal belonging to a tall, slender, dark-haired girl named Julie Bach was Mrs. Walgren's next choice. Julie had described how she'd helped with the birth of a calf. I thought what she had written was good. Really good. It belonged in the school's literary magazine—if they had one.

I slunk down in my chair as Mrs. Walgren picked up the next journal—mine. "Katherine Gillian," she said, and that friendly smile flashed again. "I've read many of her mother's articles and know what a fine writer she is. And now I can see that Katherine . . . Are you called Kate? Katie?"

I mumbled and nodded, and she went on. "That Katie has inherited her mother's writing talent and undoubtedly intends to be a writer too."

A couple of kids turned around and stared at me. I wanted to tell Mrs. Walgren she was jumping to conclusions. Why should I have to be a writer just because my mother was a writer? But I kept my mouth shut.

"Katie has reached down and written about her feelings in free verse," Mrs. Walgren said. "I want you all to pay attention to the depth she achieves and the unusual metaphor she uses."

My face grew hot, and it was all I could do to keep from groaning aloud. Nobody was going to like what I'd written.

Mrs. Walgren cleared her throat and began to read:

New girl in school?
Who says I'm new?
I'm the same sparrow I've always been,
but I've been plucked from my nest
and dropped into a town too small,
with roads too dusty and a sea too gray.

I cry out because the fall has lamed me,
but no one hears.
Gulls squabble over a dead fish,
and cluster tightly to pick the bones.
Staring with black, beady eyes
at the wounded sparrow who flaps into their unity,
they fly off in a pack,
squawking, "She's new! She's new!"
The sparrow limps alone, and no one cares.

Mrs. Walgren closed my journal, brushed a stray wisp of hair from her eyes, and nodded toward the class. "What do you think of the metaphor?"

"What's a metaphor?" Billy Don asked.

I wanted to bury my head in my hands. Billy Don was probably the only person in class who didn't understand I was writing about them.

Mrs. Walgren explained what a metaphor was so that even Billy Don should understand, but the puzzled expression on his face showed that he still hadn't got it.

Julie gave me an appraising look, then raised her hand. "I can understand somebody coming to a new school and not knowing anyone and feeling different, but I don't understand why the sparrow was lame."

"Good question. Perhaps the lameness symbolizes a feeling of inadequacy." She nodded in my direction. "Katie, would you like to explain?"

No, I wouldn't like to explain! But I had no choice. "In Houston," I said as I carefully studied the scratches in the floor, "I studied ballet in school, and I practiced the exer-

26

cises, the positions, and the movements for an hour or two every day. In Kluney there's no one I can study with."

"That *is* tough," Julie said. I looked up sharply, but there was genuine sympathy in her expression.

The boy sitting in front of me turned with a smirk, then raised his hand.

"Yes, B.J.?" Mrs. Walgren said.

"Maybe that sparrow doesn't belong on the beach with the gulls," B.J. said. "She doesn't have any business being there. It's not her territory. She needs to go back where she belongs."

Mrs. Walgren looked distressed. She opened her mouth, but didn't have time to say anything before Billy Don spoke up.

"Sometimes sea gulls can get mean, especially if you bother them while they're fighting over their food," he said. "I know a guy who got pecked all over his head. He coulda lost an eye."

"Oh, gross!" someone complained. "Why do we have to talk about sea gulls anyway?"

Mrs. Walgren glanced from face to face. In a firm tone of voice she said, "I think it's important for each of you to think about this poem and the author's use of metaphor in describing her thoughts and feelings. This is an excellent use of the journal."

She began to pass back the journals from the front desk in each row, and to my great relief, everyone's attention was diverted to the suggestions written in their own journals.

B.J. turned and shoved the stack of journals toward me with such force he slammed them into my shoulder. "Any time you want, you can leave," he whispered. "No one's gonna miss you."

I simply took my journal from the pile, then turned and passed the rest to Tammy, who was behind me.

Tammy's eyes crinkled as she leaned close. "Once Mrs. Walgren read my journal entry aloud, and someone laughed, and I thought I was going to throw up."

I realized that Mrs. Walgren was now talking about Shakespeare's *Julius Caesar* and was writing an assignment on the board, so I pulled out a pen and began copying the information into my notebook.

Just before the bell rang Mrs. Walgren said, "Billy Don and B.J., Katie and Lana Jean . . . Will you come up to my desk, please?"

Now what? I wondered, but, as the others were doing, I gathered up my books and went to stand before Mrs. Walgren's desk.

Mrs. Walgren smiled her friendly smile at all four of us, as though she really liked us. I wondered how she could. "B.J.," she said, "you and Billy Don are friends."

"Not so you'd notice," B.J. muttered.

"Nonsense. You're practically next-door neighbors, so you should be friends. But that's beside the point. B.J., I want you to work with Billy Don on his journal."

"You said what I wrote was good!" Billy Don complained.

"It was, but your entire journal is filled with descriptions of football games. I want you to expand your horizons. I want you to look inside yourself and recognize your emotions. I want you to know how you *feel*."

"That's easy. When we win, I feel good."

"B.J., you understand your assignment. Begin by trying to interest Billy Don in other topics."

She turned to Lana Jean and me. "Girls," she said, "you don't live very far from each other. I mean, it's a long walk, but it's not like you'd have to drive to get to each other's house, so I'm going to pair you off."

I must have looked as wary as I felt, because Mrs. Walgren tilted her head toward me and said, "Katie, you have a writing talent that could be shared with others. I have hopes that Lana Jean can also learn to express her feelings about a variety of topics. The topic she has chosen is so inappropriate I had to stop reading her entries. My directions and suggestions haven't seemed to reach her, so I want you to get together with her outside of school and work on her journal. It's the best way I can think of to help her get her grades up to passing."

The last thing in the world I wanted to do was get together with Lana Jean. Sure, she'd been the first to be friendly to me, but I needed my time for homework and ballet practice and to make other friends.

Lana Jean had looked hopeful at first, but now her forehead puckered, and her lower lip jutted out. "Oh, no, I can't after school," she said. "I have a job."

"What hours do you work?"

"From five to ten, all during the dinner hour." Her smile flickered timidly as she glanced at me and said, "It's at Kennedy's Grill. I work in the kitchen. They've got real good food. You and your mama ought to come by sometime."

29

I hoped their kitchen was cleaner than Lana Jean.

Shyly, she asked me, "What about weekends? Could you help me any time on Saturday? Or Sunday afternoon?"

Guilt won out. I gave up and said, "Sure. How about Saturday afternoon?"

"Fine!" A pleased satisfaction spread over Mrs. Walgren's face like syrup on a pancake. "Then it's all settled. You can work out the times yourselves." She made a little shooing motion toward the door. "Hurry, or you'll all be late to your next class."

The other three scattered down the almost empty hall, but I paused for a minute, trying to figure things out. No matter what I wanted to do, it didn't seem to matter. I was stuck here in Kluney High School until Mom's novel was written.

No alternatives. No choices. I took a deep breath and went off to class.

CHAPTER THREE

Algebra III was the first class to let out before lunch period, so I arrived before Tammy did. By the time I'd carried my tray through the checkout line there was still no sign of Tammy. Hoping she'd find me, I picked a nearly empty table, but almost immediately a tray was plopped down next to mine, and Lana Jean slid into the seat.

"Hi," she said, and began rattling on about some guy named Travis Wyman on whom she had a king-size hang-up.

Tammy and Julie came into the cafeteria. Tammy looked around, spotted me, and pointed to a table where someone was saving seats.

I just shrugged and shook my head. I couldn't suddenly

31

get up and leave Lana Jean, and I realized that most of the seats at our table had filled up.

Lana Jean, busy eating and talking at the same time, hadn't noticed. "He's a junior," she said, "and he's in Blitz."

"Who's in Blitz?" I took a large bite of macaroni and cheese.

"Haven't you been paying attention? *Travis* is in Blitz."

"Sorry. What's Blitz?" I asked, although I really didn't care.

"Shhh! Not so loud! It's a secret club," Lana Jean whispered. "Nobody's supposed to know about it or who's in it, but one night Travis was talking with B.J., who works in Kennedy's kitchen the same nights I do. Travis and B.J. were talking and smoking in the alley outside the kitchen door. B.J. left the door a little bit open, so I listened in, and that's how I know that Travis and B.J. and Duke Macon and Delmar Johnson are the members. Travis and Duke and Delmar are a year older than B.J. He was a tagalong who kind of pushed his way in, and now he acts real bossy and important when he's with the other guys."

I gave her a quick glance, but she shrugged. "Okay, so I was spying, kind of," she said, "but that's because I'm so crazy about Travis."

"I don't even know who Travis Wyman is, but I bet he wouldn't like you spying on him."

"I shouldn't have said *spying*. It's not really spying. It's just sort of watching how he walks across campus and who he talks to and stuff like that. And I keep hoping that maybe someday *he'll* notice *me.* Do you believe in love at first sight?"

"I don't know. I suppose." I poked at my flavorless red Jell-O salad and felt so sorry for Lana Jean in her impossible dreamworld that I tried to make amends. "Tell me more about Travis's secret club," I said.

"No. We shouldn't even be talking about it."

That was fine with me. I polished off something brown and lumpy that was supposed to be a bean and beef burrito and washed it down with a long swallow of Coke.

We ate in silence for a couple of minutes. Then Lana Jean said, "Guys are always having to prove themselves."

"What do you mean?"

"I don't know. That was just part of what Travis and B.J. were talking about."

"I guess we all have to prove ourselves, one way or another."

"I don't think that's what they meant."

"Why don't you just forget it? You weren't supposed to be listening in anyway. Besides, I don't want to talk about B.J. I can't stand him."

Lana Jean nodded. "Yeah. He's mean, just like his dad. B.J.'s mom ran off a few years ago and nobody blamed her, except they thought she should have taken B.J. with her to protect him from his father."

The bell rang, and I gulped the rest of my Coke, eager to get away from Lana Jean, eager to make it through the rest of the day.

* * *

I came home to find that Mom had discovered electrical outlets outside the house and had rigged up some two-hundred-watt lights. As soon as it was dark she tested them by flipping the switch inside my room near the French doors, and the yard became almost as bright as if it were daylight.

Mom looked awfully pleased with herself. She ran her fingers through her short, curly hair and said, "That ought to keep any prowlers away—that and the extra locks I installed. Did you see what a good job I did?"

"It looks great."

"I wish I'd thought of installing locks and lights while we were working to clean this place."

"I'm sorry you had to do all this stuff instead of work on your novel," I said. The sooner she finished her novel, the sooner we'd get back to Houston. "Keep working on the book!" I wanted to shout at her.

"Doing grunge work wasn't so bad," she told me. "I was stuck on a chapter anyway, and while I was putting up the outside lights the problem solved itself in my mind. I wrote the scene this afternoon, and I like it. I really feel good about it." With barely a pause she asked, "How was school today?"

"Okay," I said, and then I got an idea. "Do you have an extra spiral notebook?"

"There are five of them in the bottom desk drawer. Help yourself."

"I just need one," I said, and went off to get it. I desperately needed to put my thoughts on paper. But there was no way in the world I was going to share those thoughts with Mrs. Walgren, no matter how kind she tried to be, so I'd keep *two* journals—one for her and one for me.

I sat on the front porch steps with both journals on my lap and glanced both to the right and the left, studying the curve of shoreline in this wide, isolated bay. There was not a single house in sight, not even a fisherman or kids playing on the sand. At the moment I appreciated the peace and quiet.

In this part of Texas it was already beginning to grow warm and a little sticky, but a light breeze curled around me, licking damp tendrils of hair at the nape of my neck. The salt from the sea tickled my nose, and I wished I could run to the shoreline and dance through the foam.

Well, why not?

I tugged off my shoes, tossing them aside, and ran barefoot down to the wet, packed sand. I bent to one side, then the other, stretching to my toes, touching my nose to my knees, limbering my muscles, and testing their strength in pliés before I rose into the slow movements of the adage.

I didn't need music. The music of *Swan Lake* I carried with me in my heart, and it blended with the sucking whoosh and splash of the small waves and the rush and hiss of the foam. It rose up from my toes throughout my body —blue, green, and gold notes swimming through my head until I whirled and leaped in grand allegro across the sand, kicking up rainbow sprays as I danced and danced and danced.

A discordant sob exploded, and I realized that my cheeks were wet with tears.

The music of the dying swan soared into the broken gap,

filling it and rippling along my shoulders and arms. Remembering the final movements, I bent my head and dipped my wings, preparing to settle down upon the sand, but in the distance the Lab barked, a door slammed, and the magic vanished. I plopped onto the sand, rested my head against one knee, and gave in to the tears.

"Oh, Katie." I heard the ache in Mom's voice and quickly raised my head, wiping my eyes on the back of my hands. "It was beautiful," she said. "I watched . . . I've seen you perform, but this . . . this . . . Was it terribly wrong to take you away from your ballet lessons and your school?"

Slowly I rose from the sand and walked toward Mom. "I'll pick them up again as soon as you finish your novel and we move back to Houston." I smiled and tried to make my words light and teasing. "So stick with the writing, okay?"

"You've never spoken about wanting a career in ballet. You aren't thinking of . . . ? I mean, in ballet there must be a real dedication and hard work that can't be broken for even a day. If I thought that—"

"No career," I said quickly. "I haven't wanted to be a professional ballerina. The dance . . . Well, it's just something I . . . I like to do." I looked down and became very busy brushing sand from my feet.

What I said seemed to satisfy her. As we reached the porch she stretched her arms over her head, rolled her shoulders, and massaged the back of her neck. "We've both put in a long day, and I don't feel like cooking. Let's go out and get something to eat."

"Hamburgers?" My stomach rumbled.

"I don't feel like hamburgers. Let's try Kennedy's Grill. I heard they have wonderful barbecued chicken."

All I could picture was Lana Jean's dirty hair. "Does Kluney have a health inspector?" I asked.

"No time for jokes," Mom said. "Come on . . . I'm hungry."

Kennedy's Grill looked like nothing more than a wooden storefront on the outside, but the inside was clean and shining. No tablecloths, but the heavy oak tables were well scrubbed, and the menu wasn't too bad. There was the usual chicken fried steak and chicken fried chicken with globs of cream gravy and plenty of fries, but there were a lot of other things, too, like grilled chicken, barbecued ribs, fried shrimp, spaghetti, and baked meatloaf.

We had no sooner ordered than I caught Mom staring over my shoulder at the door to the kitchen. "I think someone's trying to get your attention," she told me.

It was Lana Jean, swathed in an oversize white cotton apron. She was leaning through the door to the kitchen, hanging on with one hand and waving with the other.

I left the table and went to see what Lana Jean wanted.

"He's out in the alley, talking to B.J.," she whispered.

"Who?"

"Travis. Come on. I want you to see him."

"Why don't you point him out at school?"

"No! Come on. Now. B.J. left the door partly open, so you can sneak a good look."

"I don't want to sneak. I—" But Lana Jean had grabbed my hand and pulled me into the kitchen.

The cooks were so busy, they didn't pay any attention to us, so I allowed Lana Jean to tug me toward the back door. She paused only long enough to jerk her head toward racks of dishes that were ready to be put into the large washing machines. "That's what I do," she said, and I felt greatly relieved.

When we reached the back door Lana Jean gave me a little shove, so I came down hard on my left foot, slapping the bare linoleum, and grabbed the open door for support.

B.J., swathed in an oversize apron like Lana Jean's, and the tall, broad-shouldered guy with him immediately stiffened, like rabbits caught in a car's headlights, and stared at me.

It was easy to see why Lana Jean was physically attracted to Travis. He *was* good-looking, with a thick head of blond, curly hair, and dark, penetrating eyes.

His unwavering stare embarrassed me. Never before had I felt so stupid. I was sure they were thinking I'd been spying on them, so I stammered, "I—I'm sorry. I was looking for the ladies' room."

"It's at the other end of the restaurant," B.J. snapped.

"Thanks," I mumbled, and quickly turned away. I heard the door slam shut behind me.

"Isn't he great?" Lana Jean whispered. She hugged her arms and rocked back and forth on her toes and heels. "You can see why I like him so much, can't you?"

"I just saw what he looks like," I told her. "I don't know anything else about him. I have no idea what he's like."

She blinked in surprise. "He's cool. Real cool. And a lot

of the girls like him, but that doesn't matter right now. I just wanted you to get a look at him."

Across the room a man yelled, "Lana Jean! Get this rack of dishes going! *Now!*"

With a conspiratorial smile and a wink, Lana Jean whispered, "I've got to get back to work," and trotted toward the dish-washing station.

As fast as I could, I dodged my way out of that kitchen and went back to where Mom was waiting for me. A couple of mixed-greens salads, swimming in ranch dressing, were already on the table.

"What's the matter?" Mom asked me. "Your face is red. Are you feeling all right?"

"Just embarrassed," I mumbled, and stuffed a forkful of salad into my mouth. "Lana Jean insisted that I take a look at her boyfriend, who was out in the alley."

"Don't talk with your mouth full," Mom reminded me, so I didn't talk at all. I was so hungry I wolfed down a large plate of fried shrimp and a baked potato before I even looked up.

Mom smiled and gave a contented sigh. "The world looks much better on a full stomach, doesn't it?"

"You bet," I said.

She signaled to the waiter for more coffee and asked, "Now, why don't you tell me more about the friends you're making at school?"

"There isn't much to tell. I've only been at school a few days. There's Tammy—who rides the bus with me—and Julie, but it takes a while to make friends."

"Don't hesitate to invite any of them over," she said.

"If they ask me first," I mumbled.

Mom didn't give me the pep talk I halfway expected. I could see she was still thinking over that dance on the beach.

"That reminds me," I told Mom, in an attempt to keep her in the here and now. "That girl you saw in the doorway —Lana Jean Willis—is coming over on Saturday afternoon. Our English lit teacher asked me to help Lana Jean with her journal writing."

Maybe just saying her name aloud made Lana Jean appear. Mom smiled and beckoned to her, and Lana Jean walked over to our table.

After the introductions and Mom saying how nice it was we were going to work on our journals together, she suggested, "Afterward, maybe the two of you would like to go to the carnival together."

"What carnival?" I asked.

"Haven't you seen the signs posted in the stores around town about the traveling carnival?"

"No," I said. "And I haven't seen the carnival either."

"It's not here yet," Lana Jean told me. "It's going to be set up on some vacant land south of town."

"Mom," I complained. "You want us to go to some kind of a kiddie carnival?"

I startled myself at how negative I sounded. Mom looked surprised too. "Don't knock it until you try it," she said. "Those traveling carnivals aren't for kiddies. The whole town usually turns out, because there are always a few rides and booths with games—things like throwing a baseball at bottles, or tossing pennies into dishes—and they're fun. It's

something different to do on a weekend night. I'm sure
that the kids from your school will be there."

"*Everybody* goes!" Lana Jean said, and her eyes crinkled at
the corners as she grinned with pleasure, just thinking
about it, I guess. "It's wonderful because—"

Mr. Kennedy hissed at Lana Jean, and she raced back
into the kitchen, not even waiting to explain the carnival's
wonderfulness. I wasn't convinced.

Mom paid the bill, and we headed for home, which
shone like a beacon. "Maybe I went a little overboard on
yard lights," Mom said, but I could tell she was as glad as I
was for all that brightness.

"The lights ought to scare off any prowlers . . . or burglars," I said. I glanced suspiciously at a dark pickup
parked just down the road. What was it doing there?

"Don't worry about burglars," Mom told me, a teasing
note in her voice. "Remember? According to the sheriff, all
criminals come from out of town."

"I don't care where they're from," I said, remembering
the footprints and the beer cans and the butt-stuffed ashtrays. "I just don't want them around our house."

As we reached the kitchen door, the outdoor lights suddenly went off, plunging us into a black hole. Blinking,
trying to adjust to the dark, I heard running footsteps, first
inside the house, then across the yard on the other side. The
pickup suddenly started up and took off fast, splattering a
burst of gravel.

For just an instant Mom and I clung to each other, both
of us thinking the same thing. Gingerly, she turned the
doorknob and slowly opened the door.

"They unlocked it from inside," she said. "So how did they get in?"

I found the answer as soon as I began looking around. The small bathroom window was wide open.

Mom, of course, had run right to her desk, letting out a screech when she saw her computer and laser printer weren't where she'd left them.

"It's okay!" I yelled. "Look! They're on the floor next to the door to the porch."

Mom sank into a chair and closed her eyes. "The novel was on my hard disk. I ran off a copy each day, but I'd made changes, and—"

"Don't worry, Mom. It's all right. They didn't take your computer. I guess we surprised them."

Mom sat up, and color began to come back to her face. "They must have run through the porch door and around the house, cutting back to the road behind the garage."

"Why don't we see what they did take?" I asked.

"Right," she said, "and then I'll call the sheriff."

We searched through our bedroom chests of drawers and closets, looked through all the kitchen cabinets, and came up with very little. The burglars had found fifty dollars Mom had stashed away, but nothing else seemed to have been stolen.

Half an hour later the sheriff showed up, walked around the house inside and out, and said, "Lucky you folks came home when you did, or they woulda made off with your computer stuff and that radio."

"What radio?" I asked.

He pointed to a small black transistor radio, with headset attached, that was on the floor behind Mom's laser printer.

I reached for it, then hesitated. "Can I touch it, or do you want to take fingerprints?"

The sheriff shook his head. "We don't take fingerprints. Doesn't do any good. Whoever did this is long gone, probably on his way to Houston. Go ahead. It's your radio. Do whatever you want with it."

"It's not my radio," I told him. I handed it to Mom. "I've never seen this radio before."

"Neither have I," Mom said. She held it out to the sheriff, who examined it closely.

Finally, he looked up. "Then where'd it come from?" he asked.

"We don't know," Mom said.

He chuckled. "Maybe the burglar left it in exchange for your fifty dollars."

"It doesn't make sense," Mom told him. "This radio doesn't belong to us, so what is it doing here?"

"Maybe the burglar likes music while he works," the sheriff answered. "You know what William Congreve wrote: 'Music hath charms to soothe the savage breast.' "

I wished he'd stop trying to be funny. I was still feeling creepy, knowing someone had been in our house while we were gone.

"I have a better idea," I told him. "The radio might have been stolen from someone else. What if the burglars hit more than one house tonight?"

"They would have stashed the haul from the other house in their car. They wouldn't carry it along with them."

I hated to admit to myself he was right, but leaving us someone else's radio didn't make sense.

"I'll check it out," Sheriff Granger said. "Let me know if you have any other problems."

It wasn't until later, when I was in bed, with all the lights—inside and out—turned off, that it dawned on me how very isolated Uncle Jim's house was. Mom had been drawn to it not only by the low cost of living, but also by the silence. No traffic, no sirens or traffic helicopter, no countless phone calls with people selling siding, carpet cleaning, or symphony subscriptions, no door-to-door salesmen or kids hawking candy bars to raise money for their schools. Here at the ocean this constant cacophony was replaced by a symphonic rhythm woven by the sea and the breeze to form a special kind of peace.

Angry at the shadowy forms who had shattered that peace, I punched at my pillow, squiggled down under the blanket, and tried to go to sleep.

CHAPTER FOUR

By the time Wednesday afternoon arrived, I'd been so busy concentrating on just getting through each day at school, I'd almost forgotten about our prowlers. When our dog-alarm went off and I heard a car pull up and stop by our gate, I automatically went out to see who it was.

A woman—she looked as if she was in her twenties—got out of the car and stood, with her hand on the open door, just staring at me. Her dark hair was tied at the nape of her neck with a limp ribbon, and her face was pale. One hand was clamped to her midriff, where her faded blue shirt met the waistband of her jeans, as though her stomach hurt.

"Hi," I said. "Can I help you?"

I saw her throat tighten as she spoke. "Does Eve Gillian live here?"

"Yes," I said. "She's working right now. Is there something I can do for you?"

"I need to talk to her," she said. "Now. I really need to talk to her bad."

Back in Houston I'd fielded phone calls so Mom wouldn't be disturbed, and helping Mom stick to her work is what I should have been doing in Kluney. The woman's skin was drawn tightly across her cheekbones in fear, and I quickly decided that in this case Mom would want to be interrupted.

"Come on," I said. "Mom's in the living room."

The woman slammed her car door and threw open our gate, nearly running down the walk. I led her through the kitchen door and into the living room where Mom was typing fast, her eyes on the computer screen.

"Mom," I began, "I hate to interrupt you, but . . ."

Mom gave a little shake of her head and looked at us as though for a moment she couldn't remember where she was. Then her eyes seemed to focus and she twisted, climbing from her chair. "Yes?" she asked. "Do you need me for something?"

"I need you," the woman answered, and she began to cry.

Mom went to her, took her shoulders, and murmured something. I was curious but I knew this was no place for me. I went out on the front porch, sat on the rough wooden flooring, and began doing my stretching exercises. In spite of the practice hours I'd been putting in, I was not in the shape I should be. *Write fast, Mom! Write fast!*

The windows were open, so the voices floated out as

clearly as though I were in the room. Not wanting to eavesdrop, I stood up, but what I heard made me sit down again.

"I'll be in trouble if they find out I talked to you," the woman said.

She blew her nose and made little snuffling noises as Mom asked, "Why?"

"Because everyone knows that you write about these things and the law gets into it and the government gets involved, and some people get hurt." She sighed. "But people are getting hurt already."

"What's your name?" Mom asked.

"Anita." Her voice had risen, as though she were going to give a last name, but she didn't.

"Sit down, Anita, and talk to me," Mom said, and the direction of their voices changed as they moved to the sofa.

"I had carried my baby only five months when I lost her." Anita's voice was so hollow, I could picture the way she had held her hand across her stomach, clutching the child who was no longer there. "And my little boy—he's five, but he doesn't play good, like a five-year-old ought to. He's always tired and he gets sick a lot." There was a pause before she said, "I tell my husband there's something wrong with the land we're on, and he tells me I'm crazy; but I'm not crazy. I seen a TV special on what they call toxic . . . toxic . . ."

"Toxic waste?" Mom suggested.

"Yes. And I read the articles you wrote about what was probably going on in Brownsville. The babies . . ." Anita's voice broke and she sobbed, "Nobody should do those things to babies."

Mom's voice lowered, and I could imagine her patting Anita's shoulder, trying to help her calm down. Finally I heard Mom ask, "What makes you think your land is toxic?"

"Just what I told you," Anita answered.

"Is it on landfill?"

"I don't know."

"Are you anywhere near power lines?"

"No. We're south of town, on a little rise that leads down to Gooley's Wash."

"I'm not familiar with Gooley's Wash," Mom said. "What is it?"

"It's a stream of sorts. Mostly it only has a little water in it, but it carries a lot of water when it rains."

"Are there other houses near you?"

"Yes. There's the Werts and the Bantrys. The Werts are gone all day, both of them working full-time at their store, but Mrs. Bantry has been poorly ever since their son moved the old couple into their new house."

"These are all new houses?"

Anita must have nodded, because Mom said, "What was the land like before the houses were built?"

"I don't know," Anita said. "I never got down there, never paid much attention."

"It was all open country? No buildings at all?"

"Oh, there's a building," Anita told her. "I thought you meant what was on our property itself. There's a company nearby that's been there for a long time. It's a waste disposal company run by the Hawkins brothers. They're the ones who built and sold the houses."

It was all I could do to keep from groaning out loud. I knew that Mom was thinking the same thing I was. A waste disposal company could mean illegal dumping of toxic waste. That would mean a red flag to Mom. But she had the novel to write, and she couldn't get sidetracked. Not now!

"Give me your address," Mom said. "We can make an appointment for you to show me around your property."

"I can't do that," Anita said, and I could hear the fear in her voice. "I thought you could just do whatever it is you do to find out about these things, and no one would know it was me who came to see you."

"Seeing the property and talking to the people who live on it is part of what I'd need to do," Mom said.

"I knew I shouldn't have come. I don't want to get in trouble."

"I don't understand, Anita," Mom said. "Who are you afraid of? Who would cause the trouble?"

"My husband, for one," Anita answered. "He's not only kin to Billy Joe and Bubba Hawkins, he works for them, as do a lot of people in Kluney."

Her voice grew fainter and I could tell that she was walking to the kitchen door. "Leave me out of it," she begged. "Please!"

"*You* came to see me," Mom reminded her, "because of the baby you lost and because of your little boy. You asked for my help, but I can't help *you* if you don't help *me*."

"I—I'll think about it," Anita mumbled. I heard the door slam and her shoes slapping the pavement as she ran up the walk toward her car.

49

As I came inside Mom dropped the hands she'd been holding to her forehead and sighed.

"I should have left the porch when I realized I could hear everything you and Anita were talking about," I told her, "but I wanted to hear. I listened in. I'm sorry."

"It's all right," Mom said. "I would have told you about the conversation anyway."

"Toxic waste in Brownsville, toxic waste in Kluney. Isn't that kind of odd?" I asked.

"Unfortunately, there are sources of toxic waste all over our country," Mom said.

"I thought there were government laws about getting rid of toxic waste."

"The laws work only when people cooperate," Mom said. She glanced at her computer screen, which was still lit, hit the save key, and turned it off. "Want to come for a ride?" she asked.

"Where?" I asked.

"I want to see Anita's house. It *must* have been built on landfill."

"And you think the landfill covers toxic waste?" I asked.

"There's a good chance," she said. "For years some of those waste disposal companies buried fifty-five-gallon drums filled with everything and anything, and the drums deteriorate and leak."

"Down to Gooley's Wash and out to the sea," I said.

Mom and I looked at each other.

"It's nothing but guesswork," I said. I was beginning to feel desperate about that look Mom gets when she's intent about something. "Anita doesn't know anything about landfill, and anyway, there's lots of landfill that isn't con-taminated with toxic waste. I think you should stay out of all this. You came here to write a novel . . . remember?"

"Anita asked for my help."

"Sure, but then she told you *not* to investigate. She told you to leave her out of it."

"I can't just ignore the situation."

"Mom!" It came out like a groan. "What about your novel?"

Mom looked pained. "For a little while it will have to wait," she said, and reached for her handbag and car keys.

The area to which Mom drove was pretty, in a way, with grassy lawns and oak trees, and the three lots Anita had told us about were good-sized. The houses, though, were simple, wooden rectangles, each of them painted white with colored trim. About a quarter of a block past them, where the road turned, was a high double fence—eight-foot cedar boards behind heavy chain link. There were warning signs to stay out, but—as we drove past the open gate—we could look inside the fence to two large brick buildings. Parked in front of the buildings were four trucks labeled HAWKINS BROTHERS WASTE DISPOSAL, and a number of cars. Judging from the depth of the fence on each side, there was a great deal of land behind the buildings too.

Mom pulled inside the gates in order to turn the car around. A guy in dirty work clothes, with at least two days' worth of gray beard, immediately popped up out of no-where and tapped at her window.

51

As she rolled it down he asked, "What can we do for you?"

Mom smiled. "Nothing," she said. "I just needed a place to turn around."

"Lost?"

"I'm headed back to Kluney."

He pointed at the road and said, "Just go back the way you came, Miz Gillian."

As Mom blinked with surprise, he gave her a humorless smile. "Seen you in town," he told her, and then he said something puzzling: "Guess Billy Joe wins the bet."

Mom didn't ask him what he meant. Hawkins Brothers Waste Disposal and Anita's house were well behind us before either of us spoke.

"He knew you," I said. "It was like they were waiting for you to show up."

"I should have guessed, just from what the sheriff told us." As she spoke, I could hear Mom's fuse growing shorter. "So many, many places, all over the country, where greedy people think, 'We'll bury the stuff and no one will care.' Well, I care!"

"Can't you just turn the problem over to the proper authorities?"

"Not yet," Mom said. "I have to get the facts. Obviously no one wants to face what's probably happening."

"Do you really think the Hawkins brothers have been burying toxic waste?"

"In this country you're innocent until proven guilty."

"But you're going to insist on looking into it?"

"Yes."

"What about your novel?"

Mom got such a longing, agonized look on her face, I was sorry I'd asked, but she said, "If it's meant to be written it'll get written."

Rats! I thought. *That isn't getting me back to Houston!* I decided there was no point agonizing over it. Usually things turned out okay.

But they didn't. Late Wednesday night the wall behind my bed shuddered and thumped as something crashed into it, exploding my dreams. I woke up so fast, I leaped out of bed off balance and ended up flat on the floor.

Mom raced into the room, scooped me up, and staggered toward the switch for the outside lights.

"What's the matter with this?" she muttered as she jabbed the switch up and down. "It isn't working."

By this time I was at the window. The moonlight wasn't much help, but I could make out enough to see a figure raise an arm high. He let fly, and a rock slammed against the side of our house. Even knowing it was coming, the thud made me jump. "They've knocked out the lights," I said. "They're still throwing rocks."

Mom turned on my bedroom light and reached for the phone. Her cheeks burned red, and she spoke angrily. "Tell him to get here now! None of this showing up fifteen minutes after they've gone!" she demanded. "I'm a taxpayer, and I want the sheriff to protect me and my daughter!"

I heard a car start up. Within seconds the shadows had shifted, dissolved, and were gone.

Mom held the phone on her lap and looked up at me with bewilderment. "Who are they?" she asked. "Why are they doing this to us?"

She didn't expect an answer, which was just as well, because I didn't have one to give her.

CHAPTER FIVE

S heriff Granger didn't have an answer either. This time Mom didn't offer him coffee. She gave him nothing but the facts.

He nosed around the yard with his flashlight and warned Mom about stepping on broken glass. "I wouldn't replace those lights," he said. "You'd just be lettin' yourself in for the same kind of trouble, long as you keep your house shinin' like a grocery store havin' a grand openin' sale."

"But the lights weren't turned on!" Mom insisted.

He frowned at her as though catching her in the worst kind of lie. "They'd have to be on in order to have kids shuck rocks at 'em."

"They weren't on," Mom said stubbornly. "Besides, what makes you think it was kids?"

"Who else throws rocks at lights?"

"You're the sheriff," Mom snapped. "That's up to you to find out."

He slowly shook his head. "No point in causin' trouble over a bunch of kids actin' up. I'll put out word I'm lookin' for 'em, and if I catch 'em their daddies will warm their britches. You won't have any more trouble."

Mom took a deep breath and suddenly blurted out, "The guard at the Hawkins Brothers Waste Disposal plant recognized me."

"Everybody in town knows you."

"This was different. It was as though they were expecting me."

"It wasn't hard for us to figure out why you were here. It's the only business around these parts you'd be interested in."

"I told you," Mom said firmly. "I came here to write a novel."

"Then what took you to the Hawkinses' company?" When Mom didn't answer, Sheriff Granger looked at her with exaggerated patience. "The Hawkinses' company gives jobs to many of the townsfolk," he said. "Matter of fact, Billy Joe and Bubba are kinfolk to a lot of the people who live in and around Kluney. As I mentioned before, they wouldn't take it kindly if you made trouble for Billy Joe and Bubba."

Mom bristled. "Just what is that supposed to mean?"

"Nothin'," the sheriff said. "Just lettin' you know how things are around here. As G. K. Chesterton said—"

"I don't care what Chesterton said!" Mom interrupted.

"What kind of a sheriff are you, quoting classics instead of catching criminals?"

"Hilaire Belloc spelled it out when he wrote, 'When I am dead, I hope it may be said: "His sins were scarlet, but his books were read." ' "

Mom strode to the door and held it open. Without another word the sheriff left.

The next day Mom replaced some of the lights with lower-watt bulbs, grumbling to herself, "I don't care *what* he said." And later that evening she put through a call to an investigator she'd worked with in Houston. "Check out something for me, will you?" she asked. "Hawkins Brothers Waste Disposal. You know what I need."

When she hung up the phone she stood next to her desk for a moment, rubbing the back of her neck, before she murmured, "I haven't had anything to do with these people, so why would they give us trouble?"

"Maybe it wasn't them," I said.

"Who else would it be?" Mom asked.

I thought about B.J., who looked at me the way he'd look at a tree roach that had wandered into the cafeteria. "The sheriff said it might be kids," I told her.

"He's wrong. Kids would have no reason to knock out lights that weren't turned on."

"They might have had another reason."

Mom studied me for a full minute before she said, "There's something on your mind, Katie. What is it?"

I told her about B.J. hoping I'd get out of Kluney. His friends, too, probably felt the same way.

"But there's Tammy and Julie," I added. "Tammy asked

me if I'd like to come home with her tomorrow and work on our history project together."

"So it isn't all bad," Mom murmured.

"The only reason I told you about B.J. was so you'd know who might have thrown the rocks. As far as school goes, don't worry. It won't be long until June."

Mom took my hand and led me to the sofa, settling down beside me. "I don't buy your idea that it was kids from your school who threw the rocks."

"Why not?"

"Some of them, like this B.J. you just told me about, may think you're a city snob, and some may dislike you just because you're different and didn't grow up in Kluney, but think about it: it takes a lot of effort to gather a group together, collect the right-size rocks for throwing, get up in the middle of the night, and risk being arrested by the sheriff."

The way Mom put it, my suspicions sounded silly, and I couldn't help smiling.

"Now," Mom said. "Tell me more about Tammy and her parents. And if you're going to visit her home I'll want to know where she lives."

Tammy and I managed to make some progress on our history project, but we mostly talked about some of the crazy things we did in junior high.

"When I was fourteen I filled out all of a sudden," Tammy said, "and I thought I was really cool, so when I saw this guy I liked coming down the walk, I leaned out the open window of our classroom and struck a glamorous pose. The only problem was I misjudged the distance and fell out the window into a ligustrum bush. The guy helped me out, and that was the end of a possible romance."

I laughed until I got the hiccups, but finally I was able to talk again. "I got so clothes-conscious I decided to come to school one day dressed like one of the models in a fashion magazine. I thought the look was fantastic, with a longish skirt and scarves around my head and neck and waist, and I had even expected people to stare with admiration. What I hadn't expected was for all the kids to laugh. It wasn't until my best friend pulled me into the girls' room that I found I'd caught the hem of the back of my skirt in my pantyhose."

"You didn't!" Tammy squealed, and we both flopped over on the floor howling and screeching.

"Is the homework getting done?" Tammy's mother called from the next room.

"Yes, ma'am," Tammy said, which made us start laughing all over again.

On Saturday, close to three o'clock, Lana Jean arrived at our house, the trio of dogs loudly announcing her coming. Her T-shirt had streaks of old makeup around the neckline, and her jeans looked like the ones she'd been wearing all week.

After she said hello to Mom, I led Lana Jean to the front porch, out of Mom's way. I said, "I'll get some Cokes and Oreos, and you can eat while I read what you've written in your journal."

"Journal?" she said, and gasped. "Oh, no! Would you believe I went off and left it on my bed?"

"How could you leave it, when that's the reason why you were coming here?"

She looked a little hurt. "Well, there are other reasons too. Like being friends."

While I fumbled for the right thing to say, Lana Jean went on, as though our friendship was taken for granted. "And I was thinking about the carnival."

Tammy and Julie had asked me to go to the carnival with them, and I'd had to turn them down because Mom had practically insisted that Lana Jean and I go together. I wasn't any too eager to go to the carnival in the first place. "Listen, Lana Jean," I said. "About the carnival . . . I really don't . . ."

She wasn't listening to me. Her cheeks grew pink as she rattled on: "I wish I could go with Travis, but of course he didn't ask me, and I don't want to go alone. What time should we get there? I wish I knew what time Travis is going and if he's going with a date or with his friends, but I don't, so why don't we get there at seven?"

She paused to take a breath, and I said, "Listen to me, Lana Jean. I don't want to go to the carnival."

"Oh, sure you do!" she cried, and the pleading in her face was awful to see. And then she said something that hit me in the stomach like a fist. "Usually I go to the carnival alone. That's not much fun."

"Well . . . okay. I'll go," I said. But I took a good look at Lana Jean and came up with an idea that made me feel a lot more hopeful about the whole thing. "You didn't bring your journal," I said, "and we've got some time to kill, so why don't we do our hair and makeup and stuff?"

"I didn't bring any makeup."

"That's okay. I've got some sample stuff from a department store giveaway that I haven't opened because it would look terrible on a redhead. There's a pink lipstick that would be just right with your light coloring."

"I guess I could try the lipstick."

"Not so fast," I said, and put on a French accent that was so bad it made Lana Jean giggle. "Madame Katherina, who does zee famous make-overs of zee stars, requires you to be putty in her hands. We start weeth a bubble bath and shampoo."

"You're crazy," Lana Jean said. "I can't take a bath at your house."

"You are not at a house. You are at zee salon of zee famous Madame Katherina. I will provide zee shampoo and bubble bath, and while you are bathing I will even wash and dry your clothes."

I guess I wasn't subtle enough, because Lana Jean looked down at her shirt and jeans and mumbled, "Okay. So they've got a few spots."

"You want to make a good impression on Travis. Right? So don't think about anything except how great you're going to look with a new hairdo and makeup and all that. I've got a blue skirt that's too tight for me to get into, and it would look terrific on you. Want to go for it?"

Lana Jean turned those trusting cocker spaniel eyes on me, as though she were willing to put her life into my hands, and said, "Will Travis think I look pretty?"

"You bet," I said, and led her to my bedroom, where I pulled out the full blue cotton skirt and sacrificed a pale blue blouse to go with it.

She was so excited about the clothes, it was hard to get her into the bathroom, but eventually she emerged, wrapped in an oversize towel. I got out some mousse, a comb, the blow dryer, a curling iron, and set to work.

Before long Lana Jean's hair fell softly around her face, turning up just a little at the ends. She watched me intently, every step of the way, and when I stepped back, saying "There. How do you like it?" she stared at her reflection as though she couldn't believe it.

"Travis will like it, won't he?" she whispered.

"He'll love it. You saw what I did. You can do it too."

"No, I can't. We don't have a blow dryer and all the other stuff."

I didn't know what to say to that, so I immediately got busy with my makeup samples and began applying some of them to Lana Jean's face.

She didn't turn out to be a raving beauty by any means, but her eyes seemed larger and her mouth prettier, and the makeup base covered most of the blemishes on her skin. I had to pull Lana Jean away from the mirror so she could get into her washed and dried bra and panties and the new blouse and skirt.

When she had finished dressing and called me into the bedroom to show me how she looked, she had the same expression on her face that Cinderella probably had when her fairy godmother got through with *her* makeover.

"I can't believe it's me!" Lana Jean squealed.

Mom came in to see if we were hungry yet for dinner, and she did a doubletake when she saw Lana Jean. "You look beautiful!" Mom said.

Lana Jean glowed. "I *feel* beautiful," she said. "And I'm not going to eat a thing because I don't want to ruin my lipstick."

"You can put on more lipstick," I said, but she shook her head.

"Not until Travis sees me," she insisted.

Mom looked at her watch. "It's nearly five-thirty," she said. "Why don't you go to the carnival now? You can get hot dogs or pizza and whatever else they're selling right there."

"That's a good idea," I said. The sooner we went to the carnival, the sooner we could come home.

"You can take the car," Mom told me. "Just give me an idea of when you'll be home."

"Eight," I said.

"Midnight," Lana Jean said.

"Compromise," Mom suggested. "How about ten? If you want to stay later, just give me a call."

Gritting my teeth, I led Lana Jean to the car. Ten o'clock seemed like a week or two away. In spite of Lana Jean's excitement, I didn't look forward to going to the carnival.

The rides and booths were set up on a large lot that had been cleared for a proposed mall that had never taken shape. The faded and torn billboard, erected near the road, still offered space for rent. Around it pickup trucks and cars were parked wherever they could squeeze in, and beyond them crowds of people swarmed under the colored lights and balloons. I parked in the only spot I could find, way down the road, and Lana Jean and I walked back to the carnival.

I should say, *I* walked. Lana Jean was so high on excitement that she was all over the place, like a little kid going to see Santa Claus.

As we reached the fringes of the carnival, some kids from school spotted her and stared hard. One even waved, but Lana Jean didn't notice. She was busy looking for Travis, and nothing else mattered.

Floating over the din of raised voices and tinny music, came the spicy fragrances of hot dogs and pizza. My stomach growled, and I realized how hungry I was. "Let's get something to eat," I shouted.

"Not yet," Lana Jean yelled over her shoulder. "I have to find Travis first. Come on!" To make sure I'd stick with her, she grabbed my wrist and tugged me in her wake.

In front of a ring-toss booth she stopped so abruptly I plowed into her, nearly losing my balance. She pulled my face close to hers and whispered, "There he is!"

Ahead of us, at a shooting gallery, stood Travis, rifle in hand, a confident leader of the pack surrounded by his friends, including my least favorite person, B.J. Behind his cloud of cigarette smoke I recognized Duke Macon, a tall, hefty, dark-haired guy who was repeating history along with Delmar Johnson. Delmar was a quiet guy who sat in the back row, slumped so far down that he rested on the back of his neck, and never got an answer right when he was called on. The three of them were egging Travis on, daring him to beat their scores, stopping only when he raised the rifle and fired.

Someone bumped into me, and I tried to edge out of the main path. "Okay, we've seen him," I said. "Now what?"

Lana Jean turned to look at me with wide eyes. "Well, now it's time for *him* to see *me*," she said. "He'll be through shooting in a minute, and we'll walk past him and say hi."

I had to think fast. I was not going to walk past that group of guys with B.J. and say *anything*. "It won't work if I'm with you," I said.

"Why not?"

"Then they'd have to talk to both of us. You want Travis to see only you."

"He'd see me," she said, but there was a question in her voice, and I jumped to answer it.

"But not as much, if he had to talk to me too."

Lana Jean took a long breath and let it out in a sigh. "Okay," she said. "I'll go alone, but where will you be?"

"Right here," I said. "I'll wait for you."

"Promise?"

"Promise."

"What'll I say?"

"What you told me you'd say. Say *hi* to him."

"That's all?"

"Unless he says something to you. Then you can stand there and talk for a few minutes."

Lana Jean straightened her shoulders and, as though there were only two people at this carnival, walked as gracefully as she could right through the crowd that elbowed and pushed around her, until she reached Travis's cluster of friends.

He was just handing the rifle to one of the other guys with him when Lana Jean stepped up and spoke.

Travis looked down at her with a kind of puzzled look and said something. I hoped he was telling her she looked great, but I doubted it.

"Hi, Katie," someone said behind my back, and I whirled around. Tammy went on. "I saw you come in with Lana Jean. You made her look good. It was you, wasn't it?"

I just nodded.

"I recognized your blue blouse."

"Where's Julie?" I asked. "Wasn't she coming with you?"

Tammy smiled and said, "She's here, and so are some other friends you haven't met yet. Want to join us and get something to eat?"

My stomach rumbled, and I giggled. "Sure," I said, but then I remembered my promise to wait for Lana Jean. I glanced at the spot where she'd been talking to Travis, but the guys had left, and there was no sign of her.

"Did you see where Lana Jean went?" I asked Tammy.

"B.J. and Travis and those other guys they hang out with went toward the rides," she said. "Lana Jean waited a minute, then I think she followed them." Tammy paused and looked embarrassed. "She's had a thing for Travis all year," she said, "and it's so obvious, everyone knows about it. Travis's been really rude to her, but that hasn't discouraged her for a minute."

"She shadows him," I said.

"I know. That's probably what she's doing now."

For an instant I was angry. She'd told me to stay here and wait for her, then she went wandering off. "Where are we meeting your friends?" I asked Tammy. "I'm getting hungry."

For a while I looked around for Lana Jean, but there was no sign of her, and no sign of Travis and his friends either. Tammy and I and the other girls tried the Ferris wheel and merry-go-round and a crack-the-whip ride that nearly brought up the hot dogs I'd eaten. I was actually having fun, and I had to admit to myself that I was glad I'd come to the carnival.

Tammy's father came to pick her up a little after ten, and I noticed that the crowd had begun to thin out. I purposefully began searching for Lana Jean, even checking all the rides, but I couldn't find her.

CHAPTER SIX

I grew more and more upset. I wanted to get out of that place, but I was supposed to give Lana Jean a ride home. If she'd gone somewhere with someone else—I couldn't imagine it was Travis—she should have let me know.

I decided to walk back to Mom's car to see if by any chance Lana Jean had gone there to wait for me. Outside the gaudy, bright circle of carnival light, the road was dark and lonely. I hesitated, waiting for others to leave so that I'd have company.

Two women and an elderly man walked past me, laughing as one of them said to the man, "Finally had enough, did you? Or do you want to go back and have a try at that crack-the-whip?"

I stepped forward eagerly, grateful to have company on

the dark road, but their car was parked close to the carnival entrance, and they drove off, leaving me standing in the middle of the road, wondering what to do next.

The plop of running feet behind me caused me to yelp and whirl, ready to defend myself, but a voice called, "Katie! Where are you going? You said you'd wait for me!"

"Wait for you!" I repeated, anger flooding out the fear. "How long did you expect me to wait? It's almost eleven! My mom is probably worried. Where have you been all this time?"

She stopped in front of me, breathing hard, her head down as though she were a child being scolded. "I thought you'd know," she said. "I was watching Travis."

In spite of the problems she'd caused me, I felt so sorry for her I couldn't stay angry. "Lana Jean, why do you spy on Travis? He must know you're shadowing him."

Her head jerked up, and she insisted, "No, he doesn't! I'm real good at it."

"But why do you want to? He isn't even friendly to you."

"He isn't *un*friendly."

"How can you say that?" I started to walk to the car, and she trotted along beside me. "Look, this is what I mean: Tonight . . . what did he say to you tonight?"

"Hi."

"That's it? Hi? Nothing else?"

"I asked him if he was having fun, and he said yeah. And then I asked if he wanted anything to eat, and he said no. And then they started to walk away, and B.J. told me to get lost."

I groaned. We'd reached the car, so I unlocked it, automatically checking the backseat, and we climbed in. "Why don't you forget Travis and get interested in some other guy?" I asked as I swung the car around and headed back the way we had come.

"I can't," she said.

She gave me directions to her house, and I let her off in front. She thanked me again for the clothes and the makeover. "I really felt pretty tonight," she said.

My impatience vanished, and I answered, "You looked great."

"Could I come over tomorrow afternoon with my journal?"

"Sure," I said. "Did you write something in it since Mrs. Walgren handed it back?"

"No."

"You'll have to write something. I know. Write about the carnival. Try to focus on how you felt about the lights, the music, and the crowds."

After an instant's thought her eyes brightened. "I will. That'll be easy to write about. See you tomorrow!" She slammed the car door and ran up the walk to the front door of the small bungalow. I waited until the door closed behind her, then pulled away from the curb.

In my rearview mirror I noticed a car without lights move out into the road. Nervously, my heart beginning to pound, I pressed down on the gas pedal, and shot ahead, eager to get home.

It wasn't until I rounded two curves and reached a straightaway that I could look back and see that no one was following me. I decided I was getting paranoid. Just because someone had forgotten to turn on his headlights was no reason to jump to the conclusion that he was after me.

Even though I tried to think rationally and calm down, as soon as I had parked the car in the garage I ran toward the house as though something were chasing me.

I burst through the door to find Mom still at her computer. "I thought you'd be in bed," I said, and locked the door.

Mom blinked, looked up, and said, "I decided while I was waiting up for you, I'd read over the first few chapters of my novel, and I began thinking about rewriting one of the scenes, and the next thing I knew . . ." She laughed, hit the *end and save* key, and turned off the computer. "You stayed longer than you thought you would, so you must have been having a good time."

I nodded. There was no point in going into my reason for leaving the carnival later than I'd planned. I babbled on about the kids I'd met and what we did until Mom gave a humongous yawn. "You're tired, aren't you?" I asked.

"I bet you are too," Mom said with a smile. "Do you want anything to eat, or are you ready for bed?"

"Bed," I answered.

Mom put an arm around my shoulders. "What you did for Lana Jean was very nice. Did she have a good time at the carnival?"

"I guess. In her own way," I answered. "By the way, she's coming over tomorrow again so I can help her with her journal."

"Fine," Mom said, and paused. "Maybe the two of you could . . . work on her journal in your bedroom?"

"I guess you could hear us on the porch," I said. "I'm sorry."

"It's okay," Mom said. She gave my shoulders a little squeeze and her eyes crinkled as she added, "The story's going well, Katie. I feel good about taking time off to write my novel." She paused and the smile disappeared. "On Monday I should get the information I requested about the Hawkins brothers' company."

I let out a long, impatient sigh. I couldn't help it. "Mom, I think you're crazy to start investigating toxic waste around here, but if it'll save time I'll help you find out whatever you need."

"I think it's better that you stay out of it, Katie," Mom said. "In fact, I just wish there was a relative I could send you to."

"No," I said firmly, hoping to stop her from thinking in that direction. She might discover an elderly great-aunt and ship me off, and it would take even longer to get back to Houston. "Mom, no matter what, I'm staying right here with you. And nothing bad is going to happen. I know it."

It was the next morning, after church services, that we heard about the murder.

The people who'd learned about it were so full of the news they even included Mom and me in the telling. Short, lumpy-jowled Belle Dobbs, who managed the drugstore, clutched Mom's arm and leaned close. "The murder victim was one of the carnival hands, according to the sheriff. Otis

73

Cantrell—you know who Otis is. He has that used-car lot on the highway to Corpus. Anyhow, Otis was out in the woods behind the carnival lot early this morning, and practically fell over the body. Like to scared him to death."

"You said the man who was killed was a carnival worker?" Mom asked. I could see Mom's investigative-reporter side emerge.

Belle nodded vigorously, then rolled her eyes and let her voice drop. "Shot right in the chest," she said.

"No one heard the shot?"

Belle's younger sister, Sudie, a somewhat plumper copy of Belle, elbowed in, shocked excitement in her voice. "One of the carnival people told Sheriff Granger he thought he heard a car backfire somewhere around eleven-fifteen to eleven-thirty, but with the noise at the carnival—the motors on those rides make an awful racket, don't you think? —no one heard anything. No one even missed him until all the people had gone and it was time to lock things up. He wasn't a regular—more a drifter who joined them just a short while back. The owner thought he'd quit without so much as a word, but that didn't seem so strange."

Mom gave a little shiver and looked at me as though she was sorry she'd allowed me to go to the carnival. "Does the sheriff have any idea who killed the man?"

Belle stepped in front of Sudie, recapturing her place as head storyteller. "The sheriff's interrogating the carnival people, and it wouldn't surprise me none if the murderer hadn't come to Kluney along with the carnival. We all know it couldn't have been anyone from Kluney."

A few others waylaid us as we walked to the car, each

repeating the basic facts of the story, with a few imaginative variations. It seems that the sheriff found lots of footprints around the body, which caused Bennie Lutz, head mechanic at the Shell gas station, to come to the conclusion that the victim was killed by a motorcycle gang.

Gibb Barker, Kluney's bald-as-a-basketball postmaster, had heard that every one of the victim's pockets had been turned inside out, everything taken, including identification. "It had to have been a pro," he said, "come down here from Houston."

As we drove home Mom murmured, "Poor man. He and another carnival hand probably got into a fight. It shouldn't take the sheriff long to find the culprit."

I felt creepy, thinking about a murder taking place so close by. I couldn't help but be glad that at the time the victim was getting killed, I was on my way home.

It was not the kind of day to dwell on a murder. The sea glittered with reflected sunlight, and the tall beach grass shimmered and shivered under a gentle breeze. I changed into shorts and ran barefoot down to the sand, letting the foam from the icy water trickle up to freeze my toes. Small, long-legged birds chased the wavelets up and back the hard-packed sand, and I watched them, trying to figure out what in the world they thought they were doing. I hadn't done my warm-ups, but even so I went through the basic positions and a few light pliés; then with my arms behind me like wings, I danced a quick, stiff-legged movement up to the foam and back, mimicking the birds.

Mom's call startled me, and I was even more startled to

see Lana Jean standing on the porch next to her. I'd forgotten that Lana Jean was coming.

As I reached the porch steps Mom said, "I've made a plate of ham sandwiches, and there's potato chips and cookies and all kinds of soft drinks on the kitchen table."

"Thanks," I said, and took a closer look at Lana Jean. She was still wearing yesterday's makeup. The foundation had turned a little orange, and there was a faint smudge of mascara under both eyes. At least she had combed her hair.

She smiled at me happily and held out a spiral notebook. "I remembered it this time."

"Let's eat first," I said. "Then I'll help you with your journal."

We munched our way through heaping plates of food before Lana Jean said, "I don't know why Mrs. Walgren doesn't like what I write in my journal. We're supposed to tell what we feel about things, and I do that."

I took a last slurp of my Coke and collected the dishes, tucking them inside the dishwasher. Mom was already typing away on her keyboard, so I motioned to Lana Jean. "Come on. And bring your journal. We'll go over it in my bedroom."

I turned to page one and began reading. Lana Jean had written about seeing Travis at a football game. "He climbed up the bleachers to the top, and as he passed me I think he saw me looking at him, so I smiled."

Skipping the rest, I went on to the next entry, which was also about Travis, as was the next and the next.

Farther on, as I thumbed through the journal, I saw that

Lana Jean had mentioned Travis's friends and their secret club, Blitz.

"This is all about Travis!" I exclaimed. "You didn't write about anything else!"

"Don't yell at me," Lana Jean complained. "I did what you said. This morning I wrote about the carnival."

I flipped to the last pages and read a detailed account of Lana Jean's arrival at the carnival, looking for Travis, and spotting him at the shooting gallery. She included their conversation and then followed his trail as he and his friends left for some of the rides.

I couldn't read any more of it. "You didn't write about the carnival. You wrote about Travis," I told Lana Jean.

"Well, Travis was at the carnival."

"Why don't you make a completely new start with your journal?" I asked. "Promise yourself you won't write another word about Travis. Skip a page, then write a description of the carnival."

She looked puzzled. "A description? Like what?"

"Like the music, for instance. Do you remember some of the tunes that were playing?"

"Not really." Trying to be helpful, she added, "But there *was* music. I do remember that."

"And there were strings of colored lights and lots of people. We stopped at the ring-toss booth. Do you remember what it looked like?"

Her forehead crinkled into furrows as she squeezed her eyelids shut. "There were prizes—little statues and teddy bears and stuff," she said, "and people had to toss rings over them."

"What color rings?"

"Red . . . I think."

"That's it," I said. "Write about what you saw, and put in lots of sensory perception."

"Lots of *what*?"

"What I mean is, tell how things smelled and tasted and felt and sounded, besides how things looked."

Lana Jean sighed loudly. "I don't know all that. This is going to be hard."

"No, it isn't," I said. "I'll help you."

"I'll get a good grade?"

"Mrs. Walgren is going to like what you write."

"Okay," she said. "I'll do it if you help me." She snatched her journal out of my hands, and before I could stop her she ripped out all the pages she'd already written.

"What are you doing?" I asked.

"Starting over. Isn't that what you said I should do?"

"You might need these. What if Mrs. Walgren wants to see the whole journal from the beginning of the semester?"

Lana Jean shrugged. "She already read this. She knows what's in it."

From the desk next to my bed I pulled out a pen and my journal—the one I was writing just for Mrs. Walgren.

"Don't write in yours. You have to tell me what to write in mine," Lana Jean insisted.

"I already told you."

"You said *what* to write, not *how* to write it."

"It has to be your own writing."

"It will be. Just tell me what to say."

I put my journal down on top of her torn-out pages and

helped her struggle through an opening paragraph describing the carnival grounds and how excited she was about being there.

She managed to write a paragraph about the ring-toss booth by herself, although she labored over it for twenty minutes.

She read it aloud, and I told her it was pretty good. It was an improvement over all that stuff about Travis.

"Am I through now?"

"You might want to say something about how carnivals make people feel."

"How could I know that?"

"Okay, then write about how carnivals make *you* feel."

"All carnivals, or just this one?"

We heard a car door slam and heavy feet stomp down the walkway. Sheriff Granger walked by, head down like a charging bull. The pounding of his fist on our kitchen door made us jump.

"Let's go see why the sheriff's here," I quickly suggested. I scooped up everything we'd left on the bed and stuffed it into my desk drawer.

Lana Jean, journal still in hand, followed me into the kitchen where Mom was standing, facing the sheriff.

CHAPTER SEVEN

"I got Harvey Boggs locked up," Sheriff Granger told Mom. "Matter of him taking a couple of punches at his wife. He says it's your fault."

Mom's mouth dropped open, but she managed to pull herself together and said, "That's ridiculous. I don't even know anyone named Harvey Boggs."

"Harvey works for the Hawkins brothers."

"That doesn't mean anything to me. I don't know him."

"You know his wife."

"No, I don't."

The sheriff pulled out a kitchen chair and thudded into it, even though Mom hadn't asked him to sit down. "You were snoopin' around the waste disposal plant, and the people there wanted to know why. Somebody seen you parked out on the road, near where Harvey and his family live. One question led to another, until Harvey's wife finally admitted to him that she'd come to see you."

Anita! I thought, and I cringed at the idea that her husband had hurt her.

"Does Mrs. Boggs need help?" Mom asked.

"Nope. She got whatever treatment Doc Foster thought she needed and went back home."

Mom's backbone grew even straighter, and she demanded, "What kind of cowardly man hits his wife?"

"A man who's afraid of losin' his job," the sheriff countered.

"That's no excuse."

"If anythin' happened to the Hawkinses' company, there'd be plenty of unhappy folks around here out of work."

"If the Hawkinses have disposed of waste products legally, then there's no reason for anything to happen to their company."

"Folks don't know why you should stick your nose into their business. The Hawkinses are doin' things right, and far as I know, get inspected regular."

I remembered one of Mom's articles exposing a crooked inspector. I wondered if she was remembering it too.

"How long have the Hawkins brothers been in business?" Mom asked.

"Their daddy started the company back in the fifties," Sheriff Granger answered.

Mom continued the thought: "Before there were laws regulating the disposal of toxic waste. You know as well as I do, all those fifty-gallon metal drums held cyanides, lead, mercury, and—worst of all—PCB's, which are now out-lawed. Those drums corrode and leak, and all the poisons are absorbed by the soil and water."

He shrugged. "You can't hold the Hawkinses account-able for whatever they did before the laws were passed."

"The houses built on their landfill aren't very old. If the Hawkins brothers knowingly built them over toxic waste, they can be held accountable." Mom was gripping her hands together so tightly, her knuckles stood out like small, white knobs. "Surely you recognize the fact that PCB's can cause cancer, birth defects, asthma—"

"Theory only. And those PCB's you're talkin' about—polychlorinated biphenyls, if I remember rightly—manu-facture of same was outlawed in 1979."

"But many electrical transformers and other products that use PCB's because they're heat-, light-, and water-resistant are still in use, or they're in need of disposal," Mom insisted.

Sheriff Granger stood. "If you want to get tangled up in government rigamarole, that's up to you, but you'll have a tough time provin' anythin' against the Hawkins brothers, and folks here won't like your nosin' around, tryin' to stir up trouble. Keep in mind the words of Douglas Jerrold: 'Some people are so fond of ill-luck that they run half-way to meet it.' "

I knew Mom well enough to expect steam to come out of her ears any minute. She snapped, "Why don't you just stick to solving your murder, Sheriff, and stop threatening me?"

"Don't get things wrong," he said. "I wasn't threatenin' you. I was just tellin' you the way things are."

"You're good at that," she said.

"And as for the murder," he said, "it's solved."

"Already?" I broke in.

At the same time Lana Jean said, "Wow! Who did it?"

Sheriff Granger barely glanced at Lana Jean and me before he nodded curtly in Mom's direction and left our house.

The next morning at school everyone was talking about the murder and what the sheriff had done, and I couldn't believe it.

He hadn't been able to come up with either witnesses or the murder weapon. The county medical examiner sent the bullet that was found in the body all the way to Dallas to a ballistics expert, but it was going to take a while to get the report. Sheriff Granger couldn't pin the murder on any of the carnival people, so he told them to clear out, to get out of town and forget about ever coming back.

That evening, during dinner, I said to Mom, "Can you believe it? He let a murderer get away. Just like that, the case is closed."

"A murder case is never closed until it's solved," Mom said. "There's no statute of limitations on a murder, and regardless of what people in this town may think, the records are available to other police agencies in other towns and cities."

"Do you mean that some other sheriff or police detective can use the information?"

"Yes. To help them solve a similar crime in their juris-diction."

"Which might mean another murder."

"That's right."

Something Mom had said suddenly rang a bell. "You said 'regardless of what people in Kluney might think'—something like that. What did you mean?"

She poked with her fork at the tuna casserole on her plate before she answered. "There was a lot of talk about the murder while I was in the drugstore. It seems that most of the Kluney people agreed with the sheriff about wanting the carnival people to just pack up and get out. As Belle put it, 'Those carny people can fight with each other as much as they want to. We just want them to take their disagreements out of Kluney and leave us out of it.' "

"What did you say to that?" I asked even though I imag-ined Mom's reaction.

"They weren't interested in what I had to say," Mom told me. "There was some very pointed talk about Anita Boggs and people causing trouble for her and everyone else. I asked if they weren't concerned about her child's health. A woman got tears in her eyes, but she said that Anita hasn't been herself since she lost her baby. They didn't want to talk about toxic waste—didn't even believe in it. Some man insisted that this toxic waste fuss was something thought up by the government to create more paperwork, and a woman reminded everyone that we didn't used to eat swordfish because the government said it had mercury in it, and now swordfish is all right. Belle slammed my purchases into a bag and wouldn't even talk to me, except to tell me what I owed."

"The woman has a point," I said.

"Katie!"

"Mom, you can't run around trying to solve other people's problems when you're supposed to be writing a novel! You don't even have any proof to go on."

Mom sighed. "You're right about that. I did get the information I requested, and there were no negative reports on the Hawkinses' company. However, they've had contracts over a number of years, with several manufacturing companies along the Gulf Coast and in Houston, to dispose of dangerous waste."

"What kind of dangerous waste?"

"Herbicides, pesticides, paint thinners, lead and mercury used in storage batteries and electrical equipment . . . There's a long list."

"Where do they dispose of these things?" I asked.

"Good question," Mom said.

I shuddered. "I don't understand why anyone would want a job collecting and disposing of toxic stuff."

"Commercial waste hauling is a highly profitable business," Mom explained. "Industries are willing to pay well to get their wastes taken away. The only problem is that it's expensive to dispose of the wastes properly, so a few waste disposal companies take the easy way out by mislabeling the contents of the drums or even involving their drivers in midnight dumping of the poisons along the sides of roads."

"Do you think that's what the Hawkins brothers are doing?"

"I don't know," Mom said. Her mouth got that tight look, which meant she had her mind set on something and wouldn't give up. "It may take time, but I've requested that an inspector do whatever is needed legally to get some soil samples from the Boggses' property."

"Why can't an inspector come right away and decide this thing one way or another?"

Mom shrugged. "There are only a few inspectors and a lot of territory to cover."

"I guess you can't just ask Mrs. Boggs if you can take some samples, after her husband hurt her."

"I actually went to see Anita Boggs," Mom told me, and I could hear the discouragement in her voice. "She was so frightened, she told me to go away and not come back."

Mom picked up her plate—she'd eaten hardly anything —and took it to the sink. "Anita has a black eye, and her mouth is swollen," she said. "I asked her if she'd like to come and stay with us, but she stared at me as if I were crazy and said there was no way she was going to leave Harvey. She even refused to press charges, so he's out of jail. I feel terrible about what happened to her just because she talked to me."

I got up quickly and put a hand on Mom's shoulder. "Don't start blaming yourself for what happened," I said. "Remember . . . *she* came to *you* because she wanted your help."

"It's pretty obvious that she doesn't want it now."

"What are you going to do?"

Mom's voice was low, but I could hear the determination

in it. "There are other people being hurt too. I can't give up," she said.

You have to give up! I thought. *You don't know for sure there's a problem of toxic waste, so writing your novel is more important!* I immediately began trying to figure out how to prove Mom wrong and send her back to her word processor, when the phone rang. It was Lana Jean.

I could hardly make out what she was saying at first, she was so excited. I almost shouted at her to slow down. She gulped a couple of times, making squeaking noises like a kitten with the hiccups, but she did manage to calm down a little.

"Katie," she said. "I did it! I really, truly did it!"

"Did what?"

"Talked to Travis. He was outside the back door here at Kennedy's waiting for B.J. I knew that B.J. wouldn't come out for a while, because the boss was chewing him out for not clearing the tables fast enough, so I just walked right into the alley and up to Travis, and this time he talked to me."

"Great," I muttered. "He said more than hi, I hope."

"So did I." Lana Jean's giggle was so excited and high-pitched, I pulled the telephone receiver away and rubbed my ear.

She was going on and on. "I thought about what you said, that watching Travis was kind of like spying on him, and I didn't want him or anyone else to think I was a spy, so I told him that I liked to watch him—the way he walks, the way he talks to people, the way he smiles kind of easy-like."

"You didn't!" I felt my face grow hot, as though I were the one who should be embarrassed instead of Lana Jean.

"Yeah, I did. I even told him about following him at the carnival."

"Didn't he mind?"

"He was kind of surprised at first, but then he wanted to hear more. I found myself telling him how I've been writing all about him in my journal, and even included the night of the carnival."

I groaned. I couldn't help it.

"Don't be like that," she scolded. "I did the right thing, because he said I was a very interesting person, and he'd like to get to know me better. He's going to take me out as soon as—"

I heard a gruff voice growling in the background. Talking as fast as humanly possible, Lana Jean said, "We're not supposed to make personal calls on the kitchen phone. I'll talk to you tomorrow."

There was a click in my ear, so I put down the receiver. It was just as well that she hung up on me, because there was nothing I could say. At first I thought about how pathetic Lana Jean was. Poor girl, she might spend most of her time in a fantasy world, but she wouldn't lie about what she told me. It was Travis Wyman I couldn't understand. He'd never noticed Lana Jean or paid any attention to her except to be rude. Then, when she finally admitted spying on him, he didn't get mad. He asked her out. It didn't make sense. I found Lana Jean's interruption very confusing, but I finished my homework, watched the last half of an old movie on television, and went to bed.

When the phone rang, I thought it was my alarm clock, and I fumbled to turn it off. While I was staring at the lighted numbers, trying to figure out why it was ringing at one o'clock in the morning, Mom turned on her bedroom light, stumbled into the living room, and answered the phone.

At this hour it had to be a wrong number or maybe an obscene call, I decided, and prepared to squirm down further under the blanket. But Mom was talking to someone, and I heard her say, "I'm sorry, Mrs. Willis. I'll check with Katie right now. If she knows anything, I'll call you back."

I hopped out of bed, meeting Mom in the doorway.

"When's the last time you saw Lana Jean?" she asked. "At school?"

"Yes, but around nine o'clock she telephoned from Kennedy's Grill," I told her. "Why?"

Worry wrinkles creased Mom's forehead. "Did she tell you anything about what she'd be doing after work?"

What had Lana Jean said about Travis asking her out? I couldn't remember all of it, but surely if he asked her for a date, it would be on a weekend. The restaurant closed at ten, and it would be nearly eleven by the time she'd finished her work in the kitchen—too late to go out on a school night.

"She didn't say anything about what she'd be doing after work," I answered, but I felt kind of scared. "What's the matter, Mom?" I asked. "Where's Lana Jean?"

Mom put an arm around my shoulders, hugging me close. "That's what her mother would like to find out. I'll call her back and suggest she try some of Lana Jean's other friends."

"Lana Jean doesn't have any other friends." As the exact words she had used came back to me, I shivered. *He's going to take me out as soon as—* As soon as what? Could it have been, *as soon as I'm through work tonight?*

"Mom," I said, fighting the hard, cold knot of fear that pressed against my chest. "I think I'd better talk to the sheriff."

CHAPTER EIGHT

Instead of the sheriff, I spoke to the dispatcher who answered my telephone call. He sounded half asleep and kind of grouchy. He listened to what I had to say, then asked, "Are you reporting a missing person?"

"No. I told you, Lana Jean Willis's mother called us, trying to find her."

"Listen, kid," he said, "your friend's probably spending the night at a girlfriend's house or, at worst, she's run away, but we can't do anything about it until her mother officially reports her missing, and then we give it three days."

"What do you mean, you give it three days?"

"We figure that with teenagers, most of 'em take off for the city. After around three days they run out of money and call home, or decide to make up with their mothers or fathers—whoever they had an argument with—or they shoplift something and get caught, and the police, wherever they're arrested, notify us."

"This girl didn't run away," I insisted.

"Okay. She didn't run away. We'll let her mother tell us that."

"If you just talk to Travis Wyman—"

"I told you, I'm not doing anything until after her mother talks to us."

"We have to do *something.*"

"The best thing you can do is get off the phone. If her mother wants to call us, she will."

I hung up, totally discouraged, and told Mom the dispatcher's reaction.

She leaned her elbows on her desk and rested her head in her hands. "I did research two years ago for the article on runaways. He's right about most missing teenagers being runaways," she said.

"But Lana Jean didn't run away!" I insisted. "She was excited about just talking to Travis and almost goofy about going out with him." I thought for a moment and said, "Mom, it doesn't make sense. Travis dates a number of really knockout girls. Why would he ask Lana Jean for a date?"

"Maybe he didn't. Maybe the date was part of Lana Jean's dream." Mom stood up and stretched, then came over to where I was standing and hugged my shoulders. "In the morning you'll find that Lana Jean has turned up safe and sound, and the only thing missing was your sleep. Come on, honey. We'd better get back to bed."

Mom was wrong, because Lana Jean didn't show up the

next day. As soon as the school bus dropped me at my stop, I decided to walk over to Lana Jean's house.

Her mother, a pale, thin-boned woman with dyed hair and orangy makeup, opened the door. I introduced myself, and she tried a smile that fluttered off her lips as soon as she began to speak.

"Oh! You're Lana Jean's friend, Katie," she said. "You were so nice . . . the way you fixed her up so pretty and the clothes you gave her. I was goin' to get around to thankin' you."

"You don't need to thank me, Mrs. Willis," I said.

"Lana Jean didn't come home last night." Mrs. Willis's fingers hovered around her mouth, and I thought she was going to burst into tears at any minute.

"I'm sorry. I'm so sorry," I mumbled.

She blinked as though she suddenly realized we were still standing in the doorway. "Come inside," she said. "Please. We can talk. Maybe you can help me figure out where Lana Jean went off to."

"Have you called the sheriff to report her missing?" I asked.

"Yes," she said. "He's here right now." She led me into a small living room crowded with large, overstuffed furniture and decorated with a collection of countless tiny china dogs that seemed to cover dozens of whatnot shelves as well as the coffee and end tables.

Sheriff Granger, who was causing the sofa to sag in the middle, looked up at me. "I was told you telephoned the office last night."

"That's right," I said, "but your dispatcher wouldn't wake you up."

"Whatever you've got to say, you can say now."

"Lana Jean called me from Kennedy's Grill. She had been talking to Travis Wyman and . . ." I stopped, unwilling to tell either the sheriff or Mrs. Willis that Lana Jean had been spying on Travis and had actually told him what she'd been doing. It was too embarrassing for her.

"And what?" Sheriff Granger asked.

I took a deep breath and went on. "And he asked her out."

The sheriff looked at me the way he probably would if I told him I'd caught a shark bare-handed. "This Travis Wyman you're talkin' about—I grew up with his mama and daddy and know Travis pretty well. Right from the day he was born Bert and Lucy tended to spoil him a mite, to my way of thinkin', but Travis is a nice enough kid, polite as they come, and real popular with all the pretty girls."

I felt my face grow hot. We both knew what he'd left unsaid.

Luckily, it all went over Mrs. Willis's head. She twisted her fingers together as she leaned toward me. "When did she say they were going to go out? When?"

Straining to remember the exact words, I said, "Lana Jean told me, 'He's going to take me out as soon as—' "

I stopped, and Mrs. Willis and Sheriff Granger stared at me. Mrs. Willis asked, "As soon as what? What's the rest of it?"

"That's it. Someone—I think it was Lana Jean's boss—interrupted her. She said they weren't supposed to use the

96

kitchen phone for private calls, and hung up." When neither of them spoke, I said, "Later, I wondered if she was going to say, 'as soon as I get off work tonight.'"

The sheriff scowled. "Are you tryin' to tell us that Travis Wyman knows what happened to Lana Jean?"

"He might."

"You're basin' this suspicion on nothin' more than what coulda been said—if anythin' was said at all."

I blushed again. "I know it seems that way, but it's still something that ought to be checked out."

He grumbled, "Which would probably amount to nothin' more than a waste of my time."

Mrs. Willis came to my defense. "Maybe the boy doesn't know anythin', Sheriff, but it could be he does. It wouldn't hurt to ask."

"I'll talk to Travis," the sheriff answered, "but it won't do any good. Knowin' Travis as well as I do, I suspect the conversation between him and your daughter didn't take place, but even if it did, maybe this young lady got it wrong."

"I didn't make anything up and Lana Jean wouldn't lie," I said indignantly. "I did get it all straight! That's why I'm here telling you about it!"

He sort of cocked his head and mumbled, " 'The lady doth protest too much, methinks.' "

"*Macbeth*!" I snapped, and probably looked as nastily smug as I felt.

"No, *Hamlet*," he said calmly.

Hamlet. Sheriff Granger was right. I probably shouldn't have blamed him for his skepticism, because at first I couldn't figure out, either, why Travis would ask Lana Jean for a date. But I was angry, maybe even a little bit at myself. The anger beat against my temples, so I took a couple of deep breaths, trying to keep from saying something I shouldn't, and got to my feet.

Ignoring the sheriff, I took Mrs. Willis's hand and said, "I'm sorry that Lana Jean is missing, but she'll come back. I'm sure of it."

Mrs. Willis stood, brushing a strand of hair from her eyes and said, "She did before."

My eyes opened wide and the sheriff sat up. "Before? You mean your daughter's run off afore this?"

"Two years ago. We had a bad argument, and she hitchhiked with a girlfriend down to Corpus. She was gone for near a week." Mrs. Willis turned pink and stared down at her feet. "I know, I didn't report it, and I suppose I should've, but it turned out all right."

The sheriff sighed impatiently as he got to his feet. "Then that's all we're lookin' at here. A runaway. How'd she happen to come home the last time?"

"She ran out of money."

"Did she have much with her yesterday?"

"Not that I know of."

"Then you should be hearin' from her soon."

"Sheriff," Mrs. Willis said shyly. "This time me and Lana Jean didn't have any disagreements."

"Makes no difference," he said. "Kids get riled about things and don't always tell their parents."

"You think that's all it is? That she's just run off?"

"I do."

Mrs. Willis's face sagged in relief, and this time a smile came to her face.

Sheriff Granger walked to the door and we followed, Mrs. Willis murmuring shy *thank-you*s, the sheriff grunting in response.

He drove off in his official car, and I walked home. It was easy for him and comforting for Mrs. Willis to think of Lana Jean as a runaway who'd soon be returning home, but I could still hear the excitement in Lana Jean's voice, her almost delirious happiness at the promise of a date with Travis Wyman, and I couldn't believe for a minute that she'd run away from that.

The next morning on the school bus Tammy wanted to talk about Lana Jean's disappearance, but I didn't.

"It makes me feel awful," I said, "like I should know where she went or what happened to her, but I don't."

"Two years ago Lana Jean ran away and was gone a week. My father said she probably ran away again."

I nodded. "Mom said most teenagers who disappear are runaways. Even the police think so."

"But *you* don't, do you? Your face shows what you're thinking."

I couldn't tell Tammy or anyone else about Lana Jean's telephone conversation. It was between Lana Jean and me, and if I were to blab it to everyone, think how embarrassed she'd be when she found out. "Let's talk about something else," I mumbled.

"Okay," Tammy said. "Have you heard about Mrs. Walgren's interpretations?"

"What interpretations?"

She smiled. "That answers my question. She's big on symbolism and drama, and every year she makes everybody in her English lit classes choose a classic and work out an interpretation around it."

"You mean act out a scene?"

"Some of them do that, but if you want a really good grade you'll think of something else."

"What else is there?"

"Last year, when my cousin Debbie was in her class, Tom Curtis got an *A* because he built what was supposed to be a mountain out of boxes and paper bags, all sprayed brown and green and white. At the top was a gold paper star. Debbie said that Tom got three of the kids in the class to lie at the foot of the mountain, looking miserable—as though they were lost, you know, in despair—and he pretended to climb the mountain, reaching out for the star."

The bus bounced over a rut in the road and I grabbed the seat in front of me to catch my balance as I asked, "What in the world book was that?"

"*Don Quixote.*"

"There wasn't any mountain climbing in *Don Quixote.* There were windmills, horses, and stuff."

Tammy looked smug. "See what I mean? It was all symbolism. Tom was struggling to reach the unreachable star, and the kids lying around the foot of the mountain were people who'd given up. He used the song from the play *Man of La Mancha,* which was based on the book."

"He must be creative."

"You're supposed to come up with something that will

make people think about the real meaning of the story, but some of the interpretations are too easy and pretty awful, and others are so weird that nobody can guess what they mean."

"Where'd Mrs. Walgren come up with such an unusual idea?"

"From Sheriff Granger. She's been in his Classical Reading Society ever since he started it."

I grimaced as I thought about Sheriff Granger. "Then I guess we'd better start thinking ahead. Did you say she lets us use any book?"

"Any classic. You can ask other people in the class to help you out, and you can use anything you want out of Mrs. Walgren's prop closet."

"What's in her prop closet?"

"All sorts of hats, fake jewels and a gold-painted jewel box, some swords and daggers, a set of black hoods, pictures, maps, a red velvet cloak . . . You name it, she's got it."

"How about you?" I asked. "Have you got something planned?"

"Julie and I have this idea for *A Tale of Two Cities*. I know we'll get *A*'s."

With a couple of bumps and a lurch, the bus arrived at the junior high, and most of the kids scrambled out. "Thanks for the warning," I said, a little disappointed that I wasn't included. "I'll start trying to think up an idea."

"You'll come up with something good," Tammy said.

Half an hour later I wished Mrs. Walgren *had* told us about the interpretation assignment. Instead, she read selections from a couple of the journals, then said to me, "Katie, did you work with Lana Jean on her journal last week?"

"Yes," I said. "On Sunday."

She nodded. "I can see improvement in her work—primarily in the subject matter—but something puzzles me. There's only the one entry. What happened to the rest of her semester's work? The pages seem to have been torn out."

Everyone in the class turned to look at me. I was particularly conscious of B.J.'s curious stare.

I attempted to explain. "She wanted to make a fresh start. She was really eager to get a good grade."

"Her intentions were good. However, it's unfortunate that she didn't remember the rules. I like my students to be aware of their progress through the semester. The last assignment is to write a critique comparing their first and last journal entry. I covered the rules of journal writing during the first week of class. You, being a new student, probably weren't aware of this particular rule, and—if so—Lana Jean should have explained it to you."

For more reasons than one I wished that Lana Jean was there to speak for herself. I wasn't going to lay the blame on her, so I just mumbled, "I'm sorry."

Mrs. Walgren didn't turn loose. "Since the pages were destroyed—"

"I'm not sure if she destroyed them. Maybe she can put them back into the journal," I blurted out, then wished I'd had enough sense to keep quiet. What Lana Jean had written on those pages was nobody's business but her own.

CHAPTER NINE

When I walked into the cafeteria at lunchtime, Tammy motioned to me to join her table. There were some other kids I'd seen, but didn't know, and Tammy introduced us. No one mentioned Lana Jean. I was grateful. They talked about the school musical, in which two of them had won parts, and the upcoming Future Farmers of America dance, which seemed to be one of the big events of the year. All I wanted to think about was the end of school, the end of summer, the end of Mom's novel, and our return to Houston. I'd been practicing warm-ups, exercises, and positions with a vengeance, but it was obvious to me that without the stimulation of the class and the guidance of my teacher I was going downhill fast.

When the bell rang I dumped my lunch trash and walked into the hall.

"Hi," Travis Wyman said. "I was waiting for you."

"For me?" I sounded like a nerd and tried to cover up by adding, "Why?"

"I just want a chance to talk to you. I think you have the wrong idea about me, and I'd like to make things right."

I swallowed a groan and tried to pretend that my cheeks weren't hot with embarrassment. Obviously the sheriff had told Travis what I'd reported about his conversation with Lana Jean. I certainly hadn't expected Travis to confront me, and I saw no need to apologize. "You don't owe me any explanations," I said.

"Yes, I do," he said, "but not here and now." He surprised me by smiling. "If it's okay with you, I'll come by your house this afternoon, after school."

As I hesitated, he said, "Please, Katie."

I stopped thinking rationally as he spoke my name with a voice that was deep and strong and soft, all at the same time. Somewhere inside my mind came the notes of a warning bell, but I ignored it. "Okay," I told him. "I get home around four."

"I know where you live. See you at four," he said, then turned and strode off toward his next class.

I barely made it to mine.

Throughout my afternoon classes I forced myself to concentrate on my work. It was the only way I could keep from thinking about Lana Jean and agonizing over the awful feeling that somehow I should know where she was. I really had to do something to find her. But what, I didn't know.

Late that afternoon, as I came through the kitchen, Mom got up from her desk to greet me, but her eyes were glassy, and she blinked a lot, looking as if she was trying to re-member where she was and what I was doing there.

"Sorry I interrupted you," I said, and tossed my books and handbag on the coffee table. "You're right in the mid-dle of a scene, aren't you?"

"Does it show?" she asked, and we both laughed.

"Go back to work," I said, "but first, there's something I need to tell you. Travis Wyman—Lana Jean's Travis—is coming here this afternoon."

"Why?" she asked.

"I guess the sheriff must have talked to him about what I told him. Travis said I have the wrong idea and he wants to explain."

"What time will he be here? Do we have Cokes in the refrigerator? Cookies?"

I gave an exaggerated sigh. "Any minute, but Mom, this is not a date. I will introduce Travis to you, then I'll take him down to the beach. You can go back to work on your novel."

"This is your house too," Mom said apologetically. "If you'd rather talk to Travis in the living room, I'll close down the computer."

"Keep writing," I said. "The sooner you finish your novel, the better."

I heard the sound of a car approaching, along with the complaints of the rottweiler, and looked out the window to see Travis climbing out of a shiny black pickup. "Here he is," I announced.

Mom snatched up the morning paper, two dirty coffee mugs, and tried to straighten up as I stood by the door, waiting until Travis knocked. He followed me through the kitchen into the living room, where Mom greeted him pleasantly.

"You've been doing a lot of research on the Hawkins brothers," Travis told Mom as he stared with surprise at the stack of printed sheets next to Mom's computer.

"That printout has nothing to do with the Hawkins brothers," Mom explained in a rather annoyed voice. "I'm writing a novel."

He didn't answer, and I had no idea whether he believed her or not. Obviously, most of the people in town didn't.

Before Mom had a chance to offer him something to eat or drink, I said, "Mom has to get back to work on her novel, so why don't we walk down to the beach?" Smiling, as though it was just what he would have suggested, Travis walked to the porch door and held it open for me.

The breeze was still warmed by the sun, and the sea, which smacked the drizzling foam close to our feet, had an invigorating sour-salt fragrance. The walk would have been pleasant if I hadn't been so nervous about why Travis had come to see me.

"This is neat, Katie," he said. "I'm sure I'd really like to be walking here with you, if we didn't have to talk about what we have to talk about."

"That's practically what I was thinking," I said, being more honest than I probably should have.

"You were?" He turned that handsome smile on me again. "Well, then let's get it over with."

Nearby was a sand bank, scattered with wisps of sea grass. Travis reached for my hand and led me to the bank, brushing off a handful of broken shells. We sat down, and I stared out silently at the pale sea, with its gold skim broken only by two oil rigs and a ship in the distance, and waited for whatever Travis would tell me.

"Part of what you said to the sheriff was right. I did talk to Lana Jean in the alley back of Kennedy's Grill," Travis began. "Only she made out what we said to be different than what was really said."

I turned to face him. "Lana Jean told me the two of you talked for a while."

He shook his head. "She talked. I listened." He paused for a minute, then asked, "Did she tell you what we talked about?"

I looked away from him and admitted, "She told you that she'd followed you a few times and—"

Anger sparked in his voice as he interrupted. "It was a lot more than a few times. According to what she told me, she was practically a spy."

"She had this big infatuation for you, but you didn't even know about it, so it couldn't have hurt. Don't get so mad."

"I did know. I heard a lot about it from some of the guys who saw her spying on me at school. They thought it was funny."

"I'm sorry," I said.

He looked down at the toes of his Nikes, scuffing them back and forth in the sand. "She told me she even wrote down everything she saw me do or heard me say in her journal for English lit class."

When I didn't answer he continued, "B.J. told me that

Mrs. Walgren asked you to help Lana Jean with her journal. I assume you probably read it. Right?"

"Only a little bit," I answered.

He straightened up and studied me. "What parts did you read?" When I hesitated, he pleaded, "You don't know how embarrassing this is for me, Kate."

"You don't need to be embarrassed," I said. "I only read the first couple of entries. I skimmed a few others."

"Did you read about the carnival?"

"Just the first couple of paragraphs. That's when I told her she'd have to write it over again and explained about description and emotion and sensory perception . . . you know, all of that."

I thought I noticed a kind of relief in his eyes, and that took me by surprise. "It's just that I ran into Cindy Jones at the carnival and . . . well, there were a couple of minutes behind the Ferris wheel . . . but it was just for fun, and if Lana Jean wrote about that, well . . . It's just not something I'd want everybody to read about—especially you. Okay?" His face turned a blotchy red.

"It's okay," I mumbled. "I don't know why you'd care what I thought about you and Cindy Jones—whoever she is."

He leaned back and smiled again, his words coming out in an easy drawl. "Now that I've met you, Katie, I really do care what you think."

It must have been the way he said my name, but I began to be glad he cared. I could understand what Lana Jean saw in him.

I shook myself back and realized I'd better stick with the

way the conversation was supposed to go. "Lana Jean told me that you said she was a very interesting person, and you'd like to get to know her better."

He grimaced and moaned, "No way!"

"And she said you were going to take her out."

Travis looked directly into my eyes and said, "If someone kept shadowing you, then cornered you in an alley while you were waiting for a friend, and told you how he followed you and wrote all about everything he saw you do and heard you say, would you tell this person how interesting he was and say, 'Let's get to know each other better'? Or go on a date?"

I didn't have to think about it. "No," I answered.

He hunched his shoulders and spread his arms wide. "There. You see?"

I nodded. "I'm the new kid in Kluney and Lana Jean was so open and kind to me, like a little kid. I just didn't think she'd lie." Now it was my turn to be embarrassed. "I was so worried about what happened to her after her mother called and said she was missing, that I tried to help. I told the sheriff that you and she had been talking, but I didn't tell him what you were talking about."

He said, "I'd appreciate it if you could keep it that way. I told Sheriff Granger that what happened was I was waiting for B.J. in back of Kennedy's Grill and Lana Jean came out and wanted to talk to me, but I brushed her off. Maybe I was even kind of rude to her. I'm sorry now if I was rude."

He looked so contrite I impulsively reached out and rested my hand on his. He sandwiched my hand between his two and said, "There's no harm done. The sheriff's known me and my family all my life, and he knows Lana Jean and her mother. He believed me." He turned my fingers so that my hand was tightly held inside his own, and bent toward me. "I hope you'll believe me, too, Katie."

I gulped. I had no reason not to believe him, except that it made no sense that Lana Jean had called me so excited she could hardly talk, then fed me a made-up story. It was crazy, but then some people might say Lana Jean's obsession with Travis was kind of crazy.

"Do you believe me, Katie?" Travis asked.

"I guess I do," I answered.

Suddenly Travis said, "Quick! Take off your shoes."

"What?"

He began tugging his off, dropping them on the sand. "C'mon. Race you along the water's edge."

"Not me!" I laughed. "The water's freezing."

"That makes you run all the faster."

He bent to grab my feet, tossed my shoes next to his, then pulled me after him down to the water, making sure I ran splashing into the nearest wavelet.

"Ouch!" I shrieked. "It's cold!"

Letting go of my hand, he raced down the beach, splashing through the shallow foam that slid up and back on the hard-packed sand. I ran after him until he came to a stop and caught me, pulling me up on the dry sand where we flopped, out of breath.

"My toes are red," I said, wiggling them for emphasis.

"It's good for the circulation."

"They're so cold they're tingling."

"Then cover them up and stop complaining," he teased, and heaped sand over my feet.

"I liked racing," I managed to say.

"It's not over yet," Travis told me. "We're a long way from your house, and we'll have to race back."

I surprised myself by adding, "I'm in no hurry to go back."

He smiled at me. "Good. Then we'll have a chance to get to know each other better. Tell me about yourself."

"There's not much to tell. My dad died six years ago, so I live just with my mom. She writes a national newspaper column and some articles for magazines, but she's always wanted to write a novel, so she took a leave of absence for six months from her job. There was no one for me to live with for six months—we haven't any close relatives, and my mom wouldn't let me stay with a friend's family—so I had to come along. If Mom can finish her novel by the end of summer, I'll go back to my school and my friends in Houston."

"Your mom really is writing a novel?"

"Really. You saw her printout copy."

"Yeah, but I didn't read what it said. Most people in town think she came here to investigate the Hawkins brothers' company. After all, she stirred up trouble in other places."

"Mom didn't even know about the Hawkins brothers until Anita Boggs came to see her and asked for her help."

"Is that what Miz Boggs did? Came to your mom? A lot of folks think that your mom went to Miz Boggs."

I sighed. "How would she know Mrs. Boggs? I'm not

111

used to a small town. In Houston something happens and no one ever hears about it. In Kluney everyone seems to know everything and anything the others are up to, even if their information is wrong."

"Folks in Kluney are interested in each other."

"Anita's husband beat her up. Everybody was interested in that, but no one seems to care."

Travis looked surprised. "Sure they care. Some of the ladies, like my mom, went to visit and brought her casseroles."

"A casserole isn't going to make up for a mean, abusive husband."

"Harvey Boggs isn't mean. He was just scared that he and all the others in town who work at Hawkins would lose their jobs. Miz Boggs didn't think about what she was doing."

"What if there really is toxic waste?" I asked Travis. "Aren't the people in Kluney afraid of living with that?"

"Nobody's proved there's any toxic waste to worry about."

I didn't want to get involved in an argument and ruin what time we had left on the beach. The afternoon shadows were long and low, and I knew we'd have to leave soon in order to be back at the house before the sun went down. The thought of Travis with me on a moonlit beach was appealing, but it seemed ridiculous as well.

As I got to my feet and brushed sand off the seat of my jeans, I asked, "Since you know everything that's going on around here, tell me about our house—who was in it before we moved in, and who was throwing rocks, knocking out our outside lights, last week?"

Travis took my hand, and we ambled along the hard-packed sand, heading toward my home. I was glad he'd forgotten about racing back. This was nicer. "I can answer the first question," he said. "No one lived in your uncle's house for over three years, but last year we all figured some beach bums had made themselves at home. A couple of people saw some strangers along the beach, but nobody comes down here much, so they didn't pay close attention."

"Beach bums . . . that's what Mom guessed and that's what the sheriff said. The house was a mess when we moved in. We really had to scrub it down."

"Aren't you glad it's a little house, with just the four rooms and a bath?" he teased. "Think what it would have been like to clean anything bigger."

I grimaced. "Those four rooms and a bath were still an awful lot of hard, dirty work." We were getting close to home and an end to our conversation. "You didn't answer the rest of my question. What about the lights? Who threw the rocks?"

"I don't know the answer to that," he said. "Kids?"

"No. It wasn't kids. Someone had been watching the house a couple of nights before that. The dogs in the properties along the road barked and woke us up, and that's how we saw the prowlers—just watching the house, hiding in the shadows, until Mom turned on my bedroom light and called the sheriff. It was creepy."

"It sure must have been," Travis said. "It sounds as if someone wants to scare you away."

"The Hawkins people?"

"I don't think so. It doesn't sound like something they'd do."

"Right." I couldn't keep the sarcasm from my voice. "I forgot Harvey Boggs. The Hawkins people are more into physical violence."

Travis threw me a sharp look. "Don't blame Bubba and Billy Joe Hawkins for what Harvey did. He's just one employee."

"You're quick to come to their defense," I shot back. "I suppose the Hawkinses are related to you too."

"Second cousins on my mom's side," he answered, "but that has nothing to do with what I said."

I had no answer. Was everybody in town going to defend or cover up for the Hawkinses? What about me and Mom?

We picked up our shoes and walked almost up to the porch before Travis stopped and looked directly into my eyes. "Have you thought about this? What if whoever had been in your house left something and decided to come back?"

"Don't!" I said as I shivered. "You're frightening me."

"I'm sorry, Katie," he said, looking so remorseful I wanted to hug him. "I was thinking out loud. I want to take care of you, not frighten you."

"It's okay," I said, although the idea still made me feel a little shaky. "Besides, if something had been left behind we would have seen it when we first cleaned the house."

"Right," Travis said. "I told you I was just thinking out loud." He smiled and added, "I didn't promise to make sense."

I could hear Mom banging pans around in the kitchen, so I took his hand and said, "Let's go in and see what Mom's cooking. If there's enough, maybe you'd like to stay for dinner."

"Thanks, but my folks are expecting me to show up for supper on time." I took a step forward, but Travis didn't budge. "Katie," he said, "According to B.J., you told Mrs. Walgren that Lana Jean probably didn't throw away the torn-out pages from her journal."

"That's right."

"Do you know where they are? I mean, since what she wrote was about me, I'd sort of like to have them."

I wished he hadn't asked. The journal pages were Lana Jean's property, and I had no right to give them to Travis or anyone else. "When Lana Jean turns up, you'll have to ask her where they are," I said.

His gaze was penetrating. "I thought you'd know."

I couldn't tell Travis I had the missing pages. Lana Jean had trusted me. I tried to make light of the situation and teased, "And you'll have to get in line behind Mrs. Walgren. Even though she told us she hadn't read Lana Jean's journal entries, she wants those papers too."

Travis followed me up the porch steps. "Can I see you again?"

"I'd like that."

Travis smiled. "I'll pass along the word that your mom really is writing a novel. That will give the gossips something to work on, and they'll stop worrying about what she's planning for the Hawkins brothers. By the way, is it a sexy romance?"

"Travis! Is that the kind of novel you think a woman would write?" I grinned at his discomfiture and added, "Tell them it's going to be a blockbuster, a best seller."

"Soon to be a major motion picture," he said.

We both laughed. "Thanks for coming over," I told him. I opened the porch door, holding it wide.

"I'll track in too much sand," Travis said, shaking his head. "I'll just cut around the other side of the house." He bent toward me, and for a moment I thought he was going to kiss me, but instead he said, "Don't be afraid, Katie. I don't think you're going to have any more trouble."

He ran down the steps and soon disappeared around the far side of the house.

During dinner I told Mom what Travis had said as he left.

"No more trouble?" Mom repeated. "I hope he knows what he's talking about. That would be good news."

Good news? I wondered, *or wishful thinking?*

CHAPTER TEN

The dogs woke us, and I heard running footsteps along the walkway, but by the time Mom stumbled into the room and we threw back the drapes at the window there was no one in sight. The outside lights allowed us just the glimpse of a car heading back up the road.

"Do you recognize the car?" Mom asked.

"It's too dark. I couldn't tell what it was. It might have been a sedan or maybe even a pickup."

I let the drapes fall back into place and shivered. "Someone ran up to the house just outside my window, Mom. He stopped for only a second, then ran back."

Mom and I stared at each other for a moment, and I could see, by the sudden fear that widened her eyes, that we were both remembering the stink bomb that had been

117

tossed into her hotel room two years ago when she was writing about fraud in one of the unions.

"Get into my bedroom," she said, pushing me so urgently that I slammed a shoulder against the door frame. "If there's an explosion, climb out the window."

"Mom! Come with me! You can't go out there! What if someone really did leave a bomb?"

Panicked, I pulled on her arm, but she pulled back, and our struggle swung us out of the little hallway into the kitchen. Mom suddenly stopped tugging, and I stumbled into her.

"Look," she said, pointing at the floor just inside the kitchen door. "It's not a bomb. It's a letter."

Neither of us moved to pick it up, watching the small envelope as though it might suddenly slither across the floor and strike.

"It's only a letter," Mom finally said, and before I could stop her she broke away from me and picked it up, slipping a single sheet of paper from the open envelope. "Short and to the point," she said, and read aloud, " 'Get out of Kluney before it's too late.' "

The crude threat was corny, sounding as though it came from an old western movie, but the anger that made someone print those words was plain and raw, and it scared me. "Do you think it's from Harvey Boggs?" I asked.

Mom shrugged. "Harvey Boggs, Belle Dobbs, Bubba Hawkins . . . Who knows? The warning could be from practically anyone in Kluney."

"Are you going to call the sheriff?" I asked.

Mom shook her head. "I doubt if it would do any good. I

can hear Sheriff Granger now, complaining that if we didn't see who shoved the warning under the door, then he couldn't do anything about it."

"What are we going to do, Mom?" I asked.

"Stay right here," she said. "I'm not doing anything wrong. I have a novel to write."

"Good! That's it, Mom—" I began, but she interrupted me with a familiar tight, determined expression.

"And this warning makes me all the more interested in discovering exactly what the Hawkins brothers are up to."

I grabbed her shoulders and begged, "Mom! Don't go to the waste disposal plant. Forget it!"

"I have to go, Katie."

"Then promise that you won't go by yourself. Take me with you. Promise me! Please!"

"All right, Katie," she said. I didn't expect her to give in so easily. "I'll pick you up after school tomorrow, and we'll drive out to the plant and see if we can get a glimpse of whatever's inside that fenced-in property that reaches from the main building all the way down to the bayou."

"That's all? Just try to get a look inside the fence?"

"It's a start," Mom said. "Even if they see us, we have a right to look."

"What do you expect to see?"

"Fifty-gallon metal drums," she answered. "Lots of them."

The next day it was hard for me to keep my mind on what was taking place in class. At lunchtime Tammy cornered me and said in a low voice, "You're a million miles away. You didn't even hear Billy Don when he said hello to you."

"Billy Don? Why would he say hello to me?"

With a shrug of exasperation she said, "Who knows? Just stop worrying so much about Lana Jean. Face facts. She ran away, and she'll probably come back before too long, the way she did last time."

I felt a little guilty, because my mind hadn't been on Lana Jean. I'd been thinking about the warning note and the Hawkins brothers and what Mom and I planned to do as soon as school let out.

"I'm sorry," I said. "I guess I have a lot on my mind."

"Well, lighten up." She nudged me.

"Hi, Katie . . . Tammy." Travis walked over to our lunch table and climbed over the bench to sit beside me. I was surprised at how glad I was to see him and flattered when Travis paid much more attention to me than to anyone else.

As the warning bell rang we scrambled to our feet, still laughing over a joke Travis had told. He stopped long enough to quietly ask me, "Want a ride home after school?"

I certainly did. I would have loved it, so the regret in my voice was real as I answered, "I'm sorry, Travis. Mom's coming to pick me up."

"I thought you rode the school bus."

"I do, but today Mom's going to be out running errands and said she'd stop by to get me."

"Will you be going right home? Can I come over?"

"Not today," I said. "I've got . . . uh . . . stuff to do . . . homework."

"How about tomorrow? Can I give you a ride home then?"

I smiled. "Tomorrow will be perfect." But something puzzled me. I'd asked Tammy on the bus that morning who Cindy Jones was, and found out she was the blond, blue-eyed, well-filled-out head cheerleader of the pep squad. With girls like that to choose from, why was Travis interested in me?

Forget the comparisons, I told myself. *Who cares about the answer?* Maybe the rest of my stay in Kluney wouldn't be so bad.

Mom was waiting for me as classes let out. I hurried to climb into the car, a little nervous now about what we were going to do.

"What if someone sees us?" I asked Mom as she drove away from the curb and through the double lines of pickup trucks.

"It doesn't make any difference if anyone sees us or not. Actually, in a place like this everyone sees everything—or everything they want to see," she said. "But we'll be on a public road. We won't be trespassing."

"You're not going inside the gates? Are you sure you don't want to talk to one of the Hawkins brothers?"

"Not yet," Mom said. "Just getting a look at what's stored on that huge lot will be enough for now."

"If there's something they don't want you to see, they may hide it."

"There's no way to hide a large quantity of fifty-gallon drums."

I told her, "You could be wrong, you know. You haven't any proof Anita Boggs is right."

Mom didn't answer, and she didn't take the route that led past Anita Boggs's house. She drove a roundabout way, following the bayou for a short distance, then heading away from it as the road made an abrupt turn. On our left, leading from the heavy stand of scrub and trees that bordered the bayou, was a high, wooden fence; and on the other side of that fence was the Hawkins Brothers Waste Disposal plant.

"That fence is at least eight feet high and solid," I said. "How are we going to see anything?"

Mom pulled the car to a stop. "I was hoping the wood would have weathered in places, or that a knothole or two had fallen out," she said. "Let's go back to where the fence begins at the bayou."

Within a few minutes she parked the car at the side of the road, under a tree with wide-spread branches, and opened the door. "Want to try climbing from the car to the tree?" she asked.

"Why not?" I smiled. "Are you coming up too?"

"Sure," she said, and pulled off her shoes.

My sneakers made it easy. The bark of the tree was rough and full of bugs, so Mom didn't try to climb it. I glanced down at her, where she balanced on top of the car, holding on to a nearby tree limb, and asked, "Can you see over the fence?"

"Just a little," she said. "I was right about the metal drums. How much land can you see?"

"It looks like acres of metal drums," I said, and wrinkled my nose. "And they smell awful."

"Are any of them corroded?"

"Yes. There's stuff oozing out around the bottom on the ones over here. The ground near the bayou is a black, sticky mess."

"Okay," Mom said. "Come on down. That's what I needed to know."

When we were both inside the car and Mom had driven back onto the road I asked, "What if the stuff in those drums is just gluck? What if it's not toxic?"

"That's a possibility," Mom said. "Tests will have to be taken. That's where the inspectors will come in."

"You said it would take time."

Mom sighed. "Yes, and it may take even more time to go through legal channels to get soil samples from Anita Boggs's property, if she and her husband are unwilling to cooperate."

"How deep would you have to dig to get the kind of samples you'd need?"

"Not deep at all," Mom answered. "If toxic waste is infecting the soil, it will seep right up to the surface." She took her eyes off the road just long enough to give me a penetrating glance. "Why did you ask, Katie? What do you have in mind?"

"Just the beginning of an idea," I said. "I haven't thought it all out, and it might not come to anything."

"Remember," Mom said firmly, "you can't help yourself

to soil samples on the Boggses' property without their permission."

"I know," I answered, but that didn't discourage me for a minute. All I wanted was for Mom to forget the Hawkins brothers and get back to her novel and finish it, so we could head back to Houston. I wanted to prove Mom wrong.

The next afternoon I rode home with Travis but didn't invite him in. "There's something I promised to do," I told him.

"Can't it wait? It's a nice day, and I thought we could walk along the beach again."

I almost gave in, but I had to find out if my idea would work. "Thanks for the ride," I said as I climbed out of Travis's pickup. "I'll see you tomorrow."

I tucked away in the trunk of Mom's car a paper bag that contained a couple of screw-top glass jars and a trowel. Then I drove to a small nursery I'd seen on the outskirts of town and bought a thick pair of gardening gloves and a flat of Scarletti begonias.

My next stop was Anita Boggs's house. Holding the flat of begonias in front of me with both hands, I managed to reach the doorbell with my left elbow.

Anita opened the door cautiously, examining both the begonias and me with suspicion.

"I brought you a present," I said. "I'm sorry about what happened."

Her face softened, and I quickly said, "I'll be glad to plant them wherever you like."

"They're pretty. That's nice of you," she said.

I fought back the guilt. "Tell me where," I said, and added, "Maybe your little boy would like to help me."

She looked away. "Johnnie isn't feeling too good today."

Still not meeting my eyes, Anita seemed to hesitate, but then she walked off the porch and pointed to each side of the steps. "Maybe you could put some along here, on each side," she said. "Do you need something to dig with?"

"No," I answered as I laid the flat on the walkway. "I brought my gloves and things with me. I'll get them out of the car."

"Thanks," she said, then glanced toward the house. "If you don't mind, I'll go back inside. I don't want to leave Johnnie alone too long."

"I don't mind," I said, relieved to have her out of the way. I collected my things, took the little plastic pots from the flat, and arranged them the way they'd look best. Then I got down on my knees and began planting.

I saw Anita watch me from the window, but she suddenly moved away. No one else was on the street, so I slipped out the first jar, filled it with soil, and fastened the top. By the time Anita had reappeared in the window, a thin little boy in her arms, I was busy planting begonias again.

The boy waved, and I smiled and waved back. Reassured, Anita walked away from the window, but I sat back on my heels, a strange, sick feeling in the pit of my stomach. No little boy should look so weak and ill. Johnnie should be out running and playing and having fun with other children. What if Anita was right about the toxic waste and

Mom was right about the need to help? One way or an-other, I felt justified in taking the soil samples.

It didn't take long to plant the begonias, and in less than a minute I had filled the second jar and deposited it with the first in my paper bag.

I was still on my knees, tidying up after myself, when a harsh voice startled me, and I jumped to my feet. Facing me was a short, muscular man. I could see he had a real attitude problem.

"What's all this? What are you doing?" he shouted.

"Harvey," Anita spoke from the open doorway. "She brought the begonias as a present. She even planted them to apologize."

I peeled off my dirty gardening gloves and stretched out my right hand. "Hi, Mr. Boggs," I said. "I'm Katherine Gillian."

His gaze didn't waver. "I know who you are." He touched the end of the paper bag with one toe. "What have you got in here?"

"My gardening stuff," I said. I was sure my hands were trembling as I picked up my trowel and stuffed it and the gloves into the bag, leaving it on the ground as though I didn't care what happened to it.

I held my breath, wondering what Harvey Boggs would do, but he didn't move toward the bag. "What did you come here for?" he demanded.

Anita took a few quick steps across the porch, toward us. "I told you, Harvey," she said. "The girl brought me the flowers. She said she was sorry about . . . about . . ."

Harvey finished the sentence his own way. "About her mother buttin' in where she doesn't belong."

I didn't say anything. My heart was pounding, and it was hard to breathe.

Harvey scowled at me, then stomped up onto the porch and said to his wife, "Get her out of here."

Just before he reached the door I got up enough nerve to call out, "Don't forget, the begonias have to be watered, and if it doesn't rain tomorrow, they'll have to be watered again."

He grunted and slammed the door.

Anita whispered, "Thank you for the flowers," and hurried into the house after her husband.

I picked up my paper bag, with the weird feeling that eyes were crawling up and down my backbone, and deliberately sauntered toward the car, afraid that Harvey might have second thoughts or decide to take a look in my paper bag. If he knew what I had in this bag, what might he do to me? I hoped he wouldn't hit his wife again because I'd come with begonias.

Suddenly, I heard the front door open, and Harvey Boggs yelled, "You . . . girl . . . hold on a minute!"

I stopped and slowly turned to face him. I was shaking inside, and I hoped it didn't show.

Glaring at me, he growled, "My wife and me don't want you here, so don't ever come back."

CHAPTER ELEVEN

As soon as I arrived home, I handed the bag to Mom and confessed what I'd done.

"Thanks for wanting to help, Katie," Mom said, "but you put yourself in danger. These samples can't be accepted in court, because there's nothing to verify them, and what you did wasn't strictly legal."

"The legal part can come along with the official inspectors," I told her. "At least this way you can find out if the soil is toxic, and if it isn't . . ." I put a hand on her shoulder and practically begged, "Mom, if it *is* toxic, I know you'll do everything you can to help Anita Boggs and her little boy, and that's what I want too. But if it's not toxic, will you please, please, please drop this investigation and stick to writing your novel? I think that's a fair deal."

"Fair enough," Mom said. "First thing tomorrow, I'll

send the samples to Houston to be tested." Then it occurred to her what I'd done and she held me at arm's length. "Take a bath and shampoo," she ordered. "Really scrub."

"Mom," I asked, "have you talked any more with Mrs. Willis? About Lana Jean, I mean?"

"No," Mom said. "The poor woman. We should call her and ask if she's heard from Lana Jean. These runaway kids —they don't realize the suffering they cause their parents, who have no idea where they are, how they're faring, or even if they're alive or dead."

I broke in. "I still don't think Lana Jean's a runaway."

"Honey," Mom said, "it's a pattern. She ran away from home before. It's very likely that she did it again."

"I know what you learned about runaways when you wrote that article," I answered, "but I still don't think Lana Jean would run away. She had no reason to run. When she telephoned me, she was so excited about going out with Travis, she was coming unglued."

"According to what Travis told you, that date with him was all in Lana Jean's mind."

"I know, but I'm really feeling torn."

"Don't you believe Travis?"

I thought about his easy, friendly smile and the way his eyes sort of lit up when he looked at me, and I answered, "I believe him, but I believe Lana Jean too. I mean, she was so crazy about Travis that she could have made up all that stuff about him saying she was interesting and asking for a date whether it happened or not, but the point is that she thought it had really happened."

"Are you sure?"

"She couldn't have faked all that excitement. Besides, she'd been honest in everything she told me about Travis. Why would she suddenly make up a story?"

Mom shrugged. "I honestly don't know, Katie."

"I feel like I should try to *find* her. The way you feel you should investigate the Hawkins brothers."

"Where? How? What have you got to go on?"

I shook my head and sighed. "Nothing. It's just a feeling."

Mom put her hands on my shoulders and looked deeply into my eyes. "I'm sure that Lana Jean will make contact with her mother or show up within the next couple of weeks, but if by some rare chance she doesn't, I'll see what I can do to help you find her."

"Thanks," I mumbled as I went off to take a bath. I was glad for Mom's help, but I wasn't satisfied. If we waited another couple of weeks, we might be too late.

Too late for what? I asked myself, anxious about the unknown.

The next morning I had just settled into my desk in English lit when Billy Don suddenly towered over me. "Hi," he said.

"Hi," I answered, looking up, up, up. He had to be the biggest guy on the football team.

"I thought maybe you were mad at me," he said.

"I'm not mad at you. Why would I be mad at you?"

"Yesterday I said *hi* to you, but you didn't say anything."

B.J. was already in his seat, his head cocked and a grin on his face as he shamelessly listened to my conversation.

"I'm sorry," I told Billy Don. "I had a lot on my mind. Tammy told me you'd said hello and scolded me for day-dreaming."

Billy Don's smile filled his broad face. "I'm glad you're not mad, because the Future Farmers dance is in three weeks, and I want to ask you to go with me."

I must have looked as astonished as I felt, because Billy Don's smile vanished, and all two hundred and sixty pounds of him seemed to sag. "Somebody else probably asked you already," he mumbled.

B.J. actually snickered, and I wished I could poke my pencil through his mean little pointed head. I hadn't given a single thought about going to the FFA dance, and I certainly hadn't imagined going with Billy Don, but B.J.'s unkindness made me so mad I heard myself saying, "No one's asked me, Billy Don. I'd like to go with you."

After I'd said the words, I wanted to crawl under my desk, but Billy Don was so happy he nearly shouted. "You would? Great! Give me your phone number! I'll call you!"

The bell rang, and Mrs. Walgren ordered Billy Don to his seat. B.J. turned to grin maliciously at me and said, "You'll be sorry. Maybe Travis was going to ask you."

I called B.J. the nastiest name I could think of and told him to mind his own business. I wondered how much Travis had told B.J. Then I realized in misery that if Travis invited me to the dance, it would be too late. I'd already promised to go with Billy Don.

Trying to think rationally, I reminded myself that the

dance would be in three weeks. By that time, according to Mom, Lana Jean would have come home, and there was no way I could go out with Travis, knowing it would break Lana Jean's heart. But Billy Don as a date? What had I done? I sighed and settled back to listen to what Mrs. Walgren was saying.

"I don't assign book reports," she said. "It's too easy—and boring—to simply write a short repetition of the plot. We have talked about the depth of meaning in the stories we've studied, so you know where I place emphasis. *Emphasis* means *importance,* and the most important part of any story, in my opinion, is the meaning the author imparts to his readers. So in your interpretations I want you to emphasize the actual meanings in the classic novels you've read."

Billy Don's hand shot up, and Mrs. Walgren said, "Interpretations simply mean what you, yourselves, interpret from the authors' meanings—what you get out of the stories."

A dark-haired girl in the front row said, "I don't get it. I mean, if the author means something in his story, then why doesn't he just say it?"

"We've talked about symbolism," Mrs. Walgren answered, and I was surprised to see that Billy Don didn't raise his hand. Did he actually understand what symbolism was? "I hope you remember that in symbolism an idea or an object often stands for something else."

The girl groaned. "I hate symbolism. It's hard."

A guy in the row by the window waved a hand. "Could I sharpen my pencil?"

"Not until I've finished explaining the assignment,"

Mrs. Walgren said. "I want each of you to understand it thoroughly, because the grade you'll get on your interpretations will greatly affect your final grade in the class."

A few of the kids groaned, and one asked if he could be excused because he had baseball practice.

"Nice try, but no one's excused," Mrs. Walgren said. "Now listen carefully, all of you, and take notes, because I'm not going to be asked four hundred times when the interpretations are due, or how long they're supposed to be, or all the other questions people usually come up with. Ready?"

Papers rustled as notebooks were opened. Two kids dropped their books on the floor, but soon order was restored and Mrs. Walgren laid down the rules.

"You will work individually in preparing your interpretation, although you may request the help of any other member of the class when you present it." Her voice became firm as she slowly and distinctly said, "We will all cooperate. If we are asked to help act out someone's interpretation, we will not refuse. Got it?"

There were only a few halfhearted groans, because she hadn't told us yet all that we were supposed to do.

"You will each choose a classic novel to interpret," Mrs. Walgren went on. "It may be one we've read in class, or it may be one you've read on your own. If you have a question about the appropriateness of your choice, you may submit the title to me for approval during the next two days."

Julie raised a hand. "Can it be something that was made into a movie?"

"You are expected to read the novel, but some very fine

novels have been made into films, so I won't rule them out. Now pay close attention," she said. "Find the deeper meaning in the novel you choose and give it your own interpretation. As you know, I appreciate drama and symbolism. You can create characters or use characters that come from the story itself to either act out a short scene or set up a diorama."

She interrupted herself to address Billy Don. "A diorama is a stationary, three-dimensional scene using props and a backdrop."

"Huh?" Billy Don said.

"I'll give you an example of an excellent diorama a student presented last year," she said, and went on to describe the *Man of La Mancha* scene Tammy had told me about, in which the song "Impossible Dream" was used to illustrate the theme of the book.

"Now, as many of you know," she continued, "I have a props closet. It's filled with things you might use in your interpretations. You're welcome to use anything in the closet—swords, capes, artificial flowers. . . . You'll find quite a collection of odds and ends, and you may bring from home anything else you might need. If you have any trouble finding the right props, come to me, and I'll help you. We will begin to present the interpretations in two weeks. Any questions?"

"The bell's going to ring," someone said, and it did.

I left English lit wondering what in the world I could do as my interpretation. I didn't have any ideas.

I told Travis about the assignment on the way home after school.

"Yeah," he said. "That's a tough one."

"She told us about the *Don Quixote–Man of La Mancha* diorama," I said. "What were some of the others?"

"I don't remember most of them. A lot weren't very good and some of them nobody understood." He turned to glance at me. "You know my friend, Duke Macon?"

"He's in my history class," I said, and wondered why Travis seemed to be studying my expression.

But the thought lasted only a second, because Travis chuckled and said, "Duke got Delmar and me into those fake swords and plumed hats. We had to be the Three Musketeers and have a sword fight."

"The musketeers didn't fight each other," I said. "I mean, they had a couple of brawls with their fists, but they were on the same side. They wouldn't fight each other with swords."

"That's what Mrs. Walgren said. Duke couldn't explain what his interpretation was about except that he thought the author liked sword fights, so he got a *D*."

"That's not much help." I leaned back against the seat and sighed. "I can't even think of what book to use."

"You're smart, Katie," Travis said, and smiled at me. "You won't have any trouble coming up with something."

"I guess I've got too much on my mind."

"Like what?" He grinned. "Me, I hope."

"I wish." Impulsively, I rested my hand on his arm and said, "Travis, I don't think Lana Jean ran away. I think something happened to her. I feel as though I should look for her . . . find her."

He slowed the pickup and pulled to the side of the road

before he turned to look at me. "Look for her where?" he asked.

"I don't know."

"The sheriff searched the alley around Kennedy's Grill and didn't turn up anything. I didn't think he would."

"Why?"

"Because B.J. told the sheriff that after the kitchen was cleaned and ready for business the next day he saw Lana Jean start walking toward home."

I began to get excited. "See! That means she didn't run away, if she was going home!"

Travis frowned as he said, "I hadn't thought about that."

"So what happened to her? She couldn't just disappear."

Travis took my hand and held it tightly. "Don't think about it, Katie. Let the sheriff work on it."

"He's not doing anything to find her."

"You don't know that."

It dawned on me what he'd said. "Besides, why shouldn't I think about what happened to Lana Jean?"

Travis shifted uncomfortably and stared out the window, away from me. "Sometimes people cut through town instead of staying on the highway," he said. "Somebody might have come along who offered Lana Jean a lift."

"She wouldn't go with a stranger!"

His voice was so low I could hardly hear it. "Or even forced her into his car."

"Are you telling me she might have been kidnapped?"

"It could be."

"But then . . . ?" I shivered, unable to finish the question.

"Katie, face it. . . . If someone did make off with her, and she hasn't come back . . ."

I began to shake. I couldn't help it. "I tried to pretend she'd be all right, but I knew! Oh, Travis, I knew!"

Travis's face twisted in agony, and he wrapped his arms around me, holding me until the tears and the torment had passed.

I pushed away, sitting upright, and said, "The woods. She may be in the woods. Take me there, please, Travis. I need to find out."

His back stiffened, and he stared at me. "That's the sheriff's job, not yours," he said, and I was surprised to see that Travis was afraid.

I probably should have been frightened, too, but sorrow and anger at what might have happened to Lana Jean got all mixed up with my guilt at hiding the truth from myself, and my own interest in Travis. All I wanted to do was prowl the woods, searching for something—anything— that might give us a clue.

"There's no point in looking for—for whatever we'd find in the woods," Travis told me, his voice cracking. "If Lana Jean was picked up—and we don't know for sure that she was—she could have been taken to Houston or Corpus or— or anyplace."

"The woods is right on the edge of Kluney," I said. "It would be easy to take her there."

Travis didn't answer, so I said, "I shouldn't have asked you to go with me. I'll go by myself, or with my mother."

Travis put the pickup into gear. "Katie, we'll go to the woods."

"You can take me home," I insisted. "I'll borrow Mom's car."

"No," he said. "I don't want you wandering around the woods alone. It's not safe."

"If you mean that whoever killed the carnival worker might—"

"I'm not talking about the carnival worker's murder," Travis said. I noticed that he looked kind of sick, and the skin around his mouth had whitened. "I'm thinking about kids with rifles out there shooting squirrels or rabbits, or even . . ." His thoughts seemed to shift and he said, "We'll talk loud and make plenty of noise. That's our best protection."

Travis parked his pickup in the dusty lot where the carnival had been pitched, and we walked on into the woods. I wished he'd picked a different spot, but in most places the heavy thicket was so overgrown with vines and scrub it was impenetrable. I reached for Travis's hand as we stepped into the late afternoon shade and discovered it was as clammy as mine. With the exception of sudden little woodland *snick*s and *crack*s, which made me jump, the woods were smothered in a deep silence.

"What about this noise we're supposed to make?" I whispered.

Travis pulled me closer to him as he stepped forward. "I'm keeping my ears open," he said. "If anybody's in the woods, we ought to be able to hear him."

Ahead of us on the path was a trampled space, with countless footprints in the moist earth, some discarded cigarette butts, and two empty beer cans.

"Let's get away from here," Travis said. He skirted the clearing, picking up speed and tugging me against some bushes that caught and pulled at my shirt and jeans.

"Wait!" I complained, jerking my hand from Travis's. Frantically, I pushed away a thorny twig that had tangled itself in my sleeve and found a fistful of black cloth in my hand. I ripped it from the twig and stared at it, trying to figure out what it was.

"Hurry up, Katie," Travis said. "We don't want to hang around here. This is where the carnival worker's body was found."

I shoved the black cloth into the pocket of my jeans and ran to catch up with him.

CHAPTER TWELVE

We followed the path for a short way, occasionally breaking into a small clearing, but more often stumbling through spreading vines that matted the uneven ground. There were no signs that anyone else had ever come this way. Finally Travis stopped and turned to face me, asking, "How far into the woods do you want to go?"

I don't know what I'd expected to find—trees sprinkled throughout a leaf-strewn clearing in a soft afternoon light? Clear signs and clues that Lana Jean had been forced to come this way? Instead, Travis and I found ourselves deep inside a dark, dank, oppressive jungle that terrified me. I slumped against a tree and mumbled, "I want to go home."

Without a word he turned, pulling me after him, and we

scrambled down the path and out of the woods as fast as we could go.

As we staggered into the empty clearing, I stopped and gulped huge swallows of air, trying to catch my breath. Travis leaned against his pickup and looked as though he'd eaten something that disagreed with him.

"I'm sorry," I told him. "I didn't know what it would be like in there." I gave a jerk of my head toward the woods. A thought occurred to me. "You said kids hunted in the woods. How?"

"There are a couple of good-size clearings with paths that lead to them," Travis answered. He opened the passenger door of the pickup. "Ready to go?"

I didn't move. "Where are the other clearings?"

He looked surprised. "One I know of is off Boyd Morris's place, and there's a kind of trail into the woods where it's not so thick about a mile or so down near the highway to Corpus. Why'd you ask? You don't want to try those, too, do you?"

I put my hands to my head, which was beginning to hurt. I had no idea what I'd been thinking, or why. It didn't make sense. "No," I murmured.

"Are you okay, Katie?"

The worry in his voice touched me. I straightened and lifted my head before I spoke. "There's no way I can search the entire woods. You proved it to me."

Travis put an arm around my shoulders. "Whatever happened to Lana Jean, wherever she is, it's not your fault, Katie. You had nothing to do with her disappearance."

"I know," I said. I climbed into the front seat and waited

until Travis had gone around the truck and settled himself in the driver's seat before I added, "She thought I was her friend. She trusted me."

He turned on the ignition and spun the pickup through a spurt of dust and gravel, bouncing over the lot and into the road. "She talked to you, didn't she, about how she was spying on me and what she heard and saw?"

"A little." I blushed, remembering that most of our conversations concerned Travis.

He glanced at me, misread my guilty expression, and said, "Or maybe you read it in her journal."

"I told you, I just skimmed parts of her journal."

"What parts?"

"Does it really matter?"

"It matters."

He was angry and trying to hide it, and that disturbed me. "Travis," I said, "I don't know why it should bother you what Lana Jean wrote about you. All I read is what I told you—mostly about how good-looking you are and stuff like that."

I had complimented him deliberately, trying to break his bad mood, but he didn't respond, so I kept on. "Mrs. Walgren said that she'd stopped reading Lana Jean's journal entries a long time ago, and I felt the same way after reading the first few. I already told you this. Don't you believe me?"

His fingers relaxed on the steering wheel, and he took his eyes off the road to throw me a quick glance. "I believe you," he said. "I'm sorry about getting so uptight. The woods . . . the place where the man was murdered . . . I guess it all got to me."

"I know what you mean. The woods were awfully creepy. I shouldn't have asked you to go there with me."

"I tried to talk you out of it."

"I know." I slid closer to him as we entered the road that led to my house. "Will you forgive me?"

"Sure," he said, and pulled his pickup to a stop where it was hidden from the house by our garage. As he turned around and faced me, his smile was so warm and deep I suddenly felt a little light-headed; so it was no surprise to me that when Travis wrapped me in a kiss that rocked me from my head to my feet, I slid my arms around his neck and eagerly responded.

When we finally pulled apart and looked at each other, the warm, glowing fuzziness between my ears vanished, and all the pieces of my mind seemed to come together again. I realized, as though I'd just come back from another planet, that it was growing dark. If Mom wasn't still at her computer, she'd be wondering where I was. "I've got to go in," I told Travis.

His smile was cozy as a cat's. "I think we've got something going here between us, Katie."

That soft way he said my name . . . I had to take a deep breath to steady myself. "Maybe," I said.

"Want me to come in with you?"

"No," I said. "Not now." Somehow I managed to open the door on my side of the pickup and slid out, awkwardly fumbling to keep my books from falling from my arms. "I'll see you tomorrow."

As I entered the house Mom looked up from her computer and squinted at me as if I were a character who had wandered into the wrong scene. "Katie?"

I turned on a couple of lights and answered before she could ask. "Mom, I'm late because I asked Travis to take me to the woods so I could look for Lana Jean."

Mom came back to reality, turned off her computer, and got to her feet, a worried frown on her face. "Oh, honey. What makes you think that . . . ?"

"B.J. told the sheriff that after work he saw Lana Jean walking toward her home." I dropped my books on the kitchen table as I said, "Mom! Don't you see? If Lana Jean was going home, then that means she couldn't have run away."

Mom put her arms around me, and I could feel the weariness in her body. "Katie, you mustn't try to work this out by yourself."

"Travis was with me."

"Or with Travis or anyone else. Wandering around in the woods isn't safe."

"You don't wander in those woods. They're all tangled up with vines and some kind of thorny bushes."

Mom held my shoulders and looked right into my eyes. "I'll be up-front with you," she said. "I talked to Mrs. Willis today. She hasn't heard from Lana Jean. I also talked to Sheriff Granger. He's been in touch with the police in Houston and Dallas. There's some indication that a paroled convict, who was on the run after committing a serious crime, came this way and headed south. He could have driven through Kluney the night Lana Jean disappeared."

My mouth was so dry it was hard to talk. "Do they think he . . . or that she . . . ?"

"He raped and killed a woman in Houston before heading south. It's a possibility that Lana Jean may have been another victim."

Everything I'd been bottling up inside exploded into tears. Mom held me, making comforting, soothing noises, until I stopped crying.

"Mom," I sniffled as I wiped my eyes and nose. "I didn't even like Lana Jean that much. But there was something about her that was innocent and trusting and helpless, like a little child. It isn't fair that someone hurt her and killed her! It isn't fair!"

"No, it isn't, but there's something else that isn't fair," Mom said, her gaze never wavering. "And that's for you to put this burden on yourself. You had nothing to do with her disappearance. There was no way you could have known about it or stopped it."

Rubbing my nose with my soggy tissue, I said, "You're right, I guess, but I still can't help feeling that there's something I should know now and something I should do. I feel guilty about Lana Jean, and I don't understand it myself."

"I'm beginning to realize how difficult this has been for you, having to leave your ballet lessons and your school and your friends and adjust to an entirely different kind of living," Mom said. "There's been a great deal of emotion involved, and I think that's what's making you feel so caught up in this problem. Believe me, there's nothing about Lana Jean's disappearance that you're supposed to know or do."

I nodded halfheartedly, and she said, "Wash your face, and you'll feel a great deal better. I'm going to make cheese tortellini for dinner. Okay?"

"More than okay." I tried a smile. "Want me to help?"

Mom grinned. "Only after you wash your face."

In the bedroom I groped through my pockets for another tissue, and pulled out the piece of black cloth I'd found in the woods. I had no idea what it was or what it meant, but I folded it and tucked it into my little jewelry box for safekeeping before I went to the bathroom to wash my face.

Mom's right. I had nothing to do with any of this, I told myself over and over as I splashed cool water against my swollen eyelids, but there was no way I could shake the creepy, uncomfortable sensation in the pit of my stomach. Maybe I wasn't supposed to get involved with Travis? Maybe there *was* something left for me to do.

On Thursday, Mom sent word to school that she'd pick me up. I knew that something was under way, so I raced out of my last class and grabbed my books from my locker. Billy Don suddenly stood in my way, as solid and wide as the front door I'd been aiming for.

"You want to go out Saturday?" he asked.

"I can't Saturday," I said. "I—I've got a lot to do."

For a minute his forehead puckered up and he said, "You're still going with me to the dance, aren't you?"

I could just imagine spending the evening dancing with this guy, while he mashed my toes with his king-size shoes, but I'd promised, so I smiled up at him and answered, "I'm looking forward to it."

He grinned like a little kid and said, "I don't go out much on dates, but my mom taught me to dance, and I'm a good dancer. I really am."

"Speaking of moms," I said. "I'm sorry to hurry off, but my mom is waiting for me."

"Maybe," he said as he stepped aside, "some time we could go to a movie too."

"Maybe," I told him, and dashed out to the parking lot.

Mom held open the door, and I jumped into the passenger seat just as she took off. "What's the rush?" I asked.

"I got the results of the test on the dirt samples you took from the Boggses' property," she said. "Toxic, with a capital *T*. I won't go into details, but it's dangerous stuff."

"Oh, no," I said. "What are you going to do next?"

"Interview the Hawkins brothers," Mom answered. She took her eyes from the road just long enough to smile at me. "Remember, you made me promise I'd take someone with me."

"That's right."

"I made an appointment with Bubba Hawkins," Mom continued. "Then I called Sheriff Granger and told him about the appointment and asked if he'd come along. He informed me that he couldn't get involved in private business matters, which is what I expected him to say."

"Then why did you ask him?"

"So there'd be a record of where I'd be, just in case."

"Mom!" In spite of the warm day, my backbone turned

to ice. "Do you think the Hawkinses would try to harm you?"

"I always take precautions," Mom said. "I even reported the time and date of the meeting to my Houston investigator."

I suppose I looked as scared as I felt, because Mom gave me another quick look and said, "Katie, I wouldn't take you with me if I thought there was any danger. I asked you to come because, primarily, I want a witness. There's also the chance that you might catch something I'd miss."

"Like what?"

"Some of my best information I've stumbled upon," Mom said. "It wasn't freely given. Sometimes it was even withheld or disguised, but people often let things slip without realizing it, or leave something in plain view simply because they're so used to it being there they really don't see it."

I thought a moment and said, "I doubt if they'll have a stack of labels lying around saying *toxic waste.*"

Mom laughed. "We may not discover a thing. However, Bubba Hawkins will. Although I obviously won't make any accusations."

I don't know what I expected Bubba Hawkins to look like—maybe a big guy in overalls and a straw hat—but I was surprised at the well-groomed, slender man in a dark blue business suit who politely greeted us as his secretary, a quiet woman who looked too young for the gray hairs at her temples, led us into his office.

"Thanks, Shirley," he said as she hesitated, studying Mom with a questioning gaze.

Shirley took the hint and quickly left the office, but I noticed she left the door slightly ajar. Did Shirley think she'd have to run to her boss's defense?

Mr. Hawkins pulled out two comfortable chairs for Mom and me and seated himself behind his large, highly polished desk. Tipping his fingers together like a tent under his chin, he smiled and asked, "How may I help you, Miz Gillian?"

At least his speech carried the familiar broad coastal accent. Glad that I hadn't been completely wrong, I began to relax.

Mom seemed perfectly at ease. "I'd like to talk to you about the toxic waste you've contracted to dispose of. How is it handled? Where is it stored?"

Mr. Hawkins's smile spread a half-inch wider. "I understand you were just down in Brownsville, trying to cause some trouble for the manufacturing companies and the farmers in that area."

Mom didn't even blink. "Have you ever seen a perfectly beautiful little baby born without a brain stem?" she countered.

"C'mon now," he said, his accent growing thicker. "Lots of things cause birth defects, such as the babies' mammas drinkin' and smokin'."

"And toxic waste infecting the drinking water."

He cleared his throat and sat up a little straighter. "Nothing got proved."

"Not yet," Mom said, "but there will be an inspection of the water for the next two years."

Mr. Hawkins actually smirked. "Is that what you're promising me?"

"Look, Mr. Hawkins," Mom said. "You know I can make enough of a stir to cause a thorough inspection of your company, even if we have to wait for it. I can also make sure that the truth about your business dealings comes out."

He had his mouth open to answer, but she broke in. "I'm not trying to put you out of business. What do I have to gain? Nothing. I'm trying to make sure that people aren't harmed by disposal being done improperly instead of properly. There are safer containers than those fifty-gallon metal drums, which corrode and leak. Landfills can be dug much deeper, and certain toxic materials can be burned, not stored."

He leaned forward, resting his clenched hands on his desk. His knuckles were stretched tautly and I could see a vein throbbing in the back of one hand, but he spoke carefully. "What do you mean, you're not trying to put me out of business? Do you have any idea how much more expensive those containers are than the metal drums? Or how much it costs to dig the extra-deep landfill? Or the high cost of incinerating materials?"

"Those costs can be passed on to the companies who hire you to dispose of their wastes."

His laugh was more like a bark. "Sure. What do you think will happen if I submit a bid twice as high as my competitors' bids?"

"What do you think will happen to people who drink toxin-contaminated water or who live on toxin-saturated land? I'm sure you've heard that the normal brain cells in the body are able to resist absorbing most poisons from the blood for a period of time. It's called the 'blood-brain barrier.' But sooner or later that barrier breaks down, and brain damage begins."

"Scare tactics," Mr. Hawkins muttered.

"Scientists have found that people infected by toxic waste suffer chromosome damage. Damaged chromosomes can mean a greater-than-average rate of birth defects and cancer. What about Anita Boggs and her family, and the others who live in the houses built over your landfill? Are you willing to cause such suffering to them?"

Mr. Hawkins angrily jumped to his feet. "Get off my back! I don't know why you picked our company to attack, when nobody around here's been hurt or even had cause to complain, exceptin' Miz Boggs, whose mind went kind of strange after she lost her baby. But you can't lay that on me!" His voice grew louder, and his face turned red. "You want crooked companies cheatin' on toxic waste disposal? I can give you names! Midnight haulers who drive to remote areas and dump the stuff at the sides of the roads, or in bayous where no one will know! Companies who sell contaminated oil to lay on roads or use as fuel! You want names?"

"Yes," Mom said quietly as she took a notebook and pen out of her handbag, "I do."

Mr. Hawkins stopped abruptly, flopping into his chair. He poured himself a glass of water from a carafe on his desk and stirred through his desk drawer until he pulled out a bottle of pills, dumped a couple into one hand and popped them into his mouth. He took a long drink of water before he calmly answered, "You got me upset, and when I get upset I talk too much. I've got nothing more to say."

"You aren't going to give me the names?"

"What names?"

"There's no reason to single *you* out. *All* the waste disposal companies should obey the laws."

Mr. Hawkins didn't answer. He and Mom just stared at each other for a couple of minutes. Then Mom said, "Before we leave, may I get a look at the drums you have stored behind this building?"

His smile barely sneaked onto his face. "Why? So you can see how they're labeled?"

Mom nodded, and Mr. Hawkins laughed. "Sure, you can see the ones close by if you want, and you'll find their labels are all in order. I can't let you down into the lot, though, because you'd ruin your pretty clothes."

"I understand," Mom said without a hint of sarcasm.

He looked surprised, but stood and motioned us to follow him.

As he led us through his outer office I noticed Shirley get up from her desk and watch us pass. I saw that her face looked as if she were watching a funeral procession. *Whose funeral?* I thought.

We walked through the building with people either staring or glaring at us. Out at the back, we stood on a sort of loading dock. We could see for quite a distance down the low, sloping hill—every scrap of space covered with metal drums.

Mom had her handbag clutched to her chest. She slowly

looked around, facing first one direction then the other. I was careful not only to keep out of her way but to keep Mr. Hawkins from getting in front of the hidden camera Mom had put inside her handbag. It was a clear day, and she was going to get some good pictures, which could easily be enlarged.

Impatiently, Mr. Hawkins ushered us down concrete steps and across a driveway to an area in which fifty-gallon drums were arranged in neat rows that stretched half a block wide. "Take a look at the labels," he said.

Mom obediently looked and secretly snapped her photos. I looked, too, but label after label listed the contents as iron filings from some manufacturing company. "Iron filings?" Mom said. "What else is in these drums?"

"Iron filings," Mr. Hawkins said with a grin.

"I got a glimpse of the drums down at the foot of your property," Mom told him. "They were corroded and oozing something that wasn't from iron filings. Have you got anything here that's correctly labeled? Such as contaminated fuel oil from the chain of garages you haul waste from? Maybe radiator coolants? Or Freon from air conditioners?"

Mr. Hawkins's manner changed abruptly. "I think you've been here long enough, Miz Gillian," he said. He put one hand on Mom's right elbow and one hand on my left elbow and propelled us up the steps, through the building, and out the front door. People stopped their work to watch, and a couple of them followed us to the open doorway. Shirley was among them, and for the first time I thought I understood the expression on her face.

"Don't ask for any more cooperation," Mr. Hawkins told Mom, "because you aren't going to get it."

"Thank you for the help you *did* give me," Mom said formally.

He took a step toward her and lowered his voice. "In case you've got a tape recorder going, which I wouldn't put past you, I want to make clear that what I'm going to say isn't a threat. It's the simple truth. There are plenty of folks in town who depend on our company for jobs. If we're put out of business the whole town's going to suffer. The people of Kluney don't take kindly to what you're trying to do to us."

Mom's back stiffened. "I'm not trying to put your company out of business. I'm simply trying to get you to run an efficient, *legal* operation. Think about what you're doing to your fellow townspeople. Slowly, but surely, you're killing them. You have your responsibilities, and I have mine. I know I can live with my conscience."

Mr. Hawkins didn't answer. He just gave Mom the hardest, meanest stare I've ever seen one person give another. Mom didn't flinch, but I was scared. All I wanted was to get away from that place as fast as possible!

CHAPTER THIRTEEN

On the way home I asked Mom, "Do you think the labels on the drums were phony?"

"Not on the drums we saw close at hand," Mom said. "But it stands to reason that the Hawkinses wouldn't keep toxic waste close to the place where they work." She sighed. "It's going to be a long, hard job to get the Hawkins brothers' company to shape up."

I thought again about Shirley. "What if you got some help from Bubba Hawkins's secretary?"

Mom looked at me sharply. "Shirley? Did she say or do anything to give you the idea she'd help?"

"It was the expression on her face," I said, "and the way she listened in to our conversation. At first I thought she was ready to protect Bubba Hawkins, but I changed my mind when I saw the look in her eyes. I think she was scared, Mom, and I know she was really unhappy."

Mom smiled at me. "Thanks for picking up on that," she said. "You'd make a good reporter, Katie."

"Thanks, but no thanks," I told her.

"Tomorrow morning," Mom said, "I'll take a plane to Austin. There are some state officials there who need to hear what I have to tell them. I can catch a commuter flight from Hunterville and be back by dinnertime." She glanced at me again. "Will that be all right with you, Katie? You'll be okay while I'm gone?"

I laughed. "Mom, I'm not five years old. I can take care of myself all day long. Honest! Besides, it's Friday. During most of the day I'll be at school."

The air was thick and muggy the next morning, and I didn't envy Mom her hour-plus flight in a small prop plane that would probably bounce all the way to Austin.

On the school bus Tammy expressed surprise that I'd go to the Future Farmers dance with Billy Don. "He's not exactly the brightest guy in the world," she said, and we both giggled.

I winced as we went over a bump and bounced against the uncomfortable seat. "I agreed to go with Billy Don because of B.J.," I admitted. "B.J. was smirking and snickering and made me so mad, because I thought he'd hurt Billy Don's feelings. So I told Billy Don I'd go with him, and then I wished I hadn't, but it doesn't make that much difference, because no one else is going to ask me anyway."

"I thought Travis might."

"Well, he hasn't."

"What if he does?"

I had to change the subject. "Are you going?"

"Laura told Julie that Stan told Marcus he was going to ask me." Tammy went on, explaining the chain of gossip.

Everyone at school seemed to be in a good mood—even B.J. News got around fast that the night before, a fight had taken place between two carnival workers down in Harlingen. One had shot the other and was being held on murder charges. Since it was the same carnival that had been in Kluney, Sheriff Granger was crowing about being right. "It's out-of-towners causin' all the trouble," he'd told the local radio reporter, who expressed the opinion that now everyone in Kluney could relax.

But what about Lana Jean? I thought.

By the time I got home the weather was even worse, and by five o'clock a drippy fog had crept in from the sea. The phone rang, and I knew before answering that it was Mom.

Her voice was high-pitched with worry as she said, "Katie, I've been sitting in Austin for a couple of hours while the pilot waited to see if the weather would clear up. Now he tells me that the coast is fogged in, and he can't fly back to Hunterville until the fog lifts sometime tomorrow morning."

I didn't like the news any more than she did, but I said, "Don't worry about me, Mom. I'll be okay."

"I shouldn't have come," she said. "I had no business leaving you there alone, especially after . . ."

I had to interrupt. What she said was scaring me. "Mom, hold on! You had no way of knowing we'd get fogged in.

159

And it's silly to worry about what might happen. Nothing's going to happen. I promise."

Obviously, Mom wasn't counting on empty promises. "I've been thinking, Katie," she said. "Can you ask Tammy to spend the night with you? Or go to her house?"

An immense feeling of relief swept through me. "Sure," I said. "No problem, Mom."

"Good," she said, and I could hear her begin to relax. "Write down this number in case you need to get in touch with me. I'll be at the Sheraton."

I did as she said, and as soon as she finished asking me a million times if I'd be all right I said good night, hung up the phone, and immediately called Tammy.

It was Tammy's mother I spoke to, not Tammy, who had gone to visit her aunt for the weekend.

"I'll tell her you called," Mrs. Ludd said. "She'll be back Sunday evening."

I thanked Mrs. Ludd and hung up, nervously staring out the windows at the white soup that pushed against the glass. I telephoned Julie, who was sick with a twenty-four–hour virus, and two other girls who often ended up at our lunch table, but they were baby-sitting.

"It's crazy to be scared," I said aloud, trying to talk myself into a better frame of mind. It was a known fact that the full moon, not fog, brought out the weirdos. And on such a damp, miserable night, wouldn't even the weirdos want to stay indoors like everybody else? Sure they would.

After I'd turned on all the lights in the house, I heated a can of soup and ate it with a stack of crackers. On a full stomach, the situation looked much better. It was Friday night, however, and I didn't want to do homework. I tried a couple of shows on television, but didn't like either of them. I was going to call Mom, just to talk to someone, but I didn't want to worry her.

I was just beginning to feel desperate, and was going to write in my journal, when I remembered the pages from Lana Jean's journal. I don't know why, but I felt a compulsion to read them. I settled on the living room sofa and began reading from where I'd once given up.

Everything Lana Jean had written was about Travis—the people he talked to and even things he'd said, when she'd been close enough to overhear. If she'd told Travis even half of what she'd written about him, I could see why he'd want to destroy these pages.

Since Travis was usually with his friends, B.J., Duke, and Delmar, Lana Jean had a few comments about them too. She thought B.J. was as mean and bossy as his father, if not more so; Duke was a show-off, always trying to impress all the girls; and Delmar didn't think for himself, content to do everything the others told him to do.

"They made up a club called Blitz," she wrote, "and nobody else can be in it, and they can't be in it either unless they follow all the rules, which go one, two, three, four, five, getting harder all the time, and if you don't you're out, which is all I heard."

I could see why Mrs. Walgren had bailed out. I read that paragraph over three times and still couldn't quite figure out what Lana Jean was writing about.

I was into the next page, reading about what Travis had eaten for lunch, when I realized the rottweiler was barking furiously, with the other two dogs backing him up. I became totally alert. There was a squeak as our gate was opened and slow, steady footfalls padded along the walkway.

Frantically, I lifted a cushion from the sofa and hid Lana Jean's papers under it. I tiptoed into the kitchen, opened one of the drawers, pulled out Mom's largest butcher knife, and then waited. My heart was banging in my chest as I heard the footsteps stop outside our kitchen door.

A loud knock on the door made me jump.

"Who's there?" I asked in a whisper. I cleared my throat and shouted this time, "Who's there?"

"It's me, Katie . . . Travis," came the answer.

Grunting with relief, I tossed the knife back inside the drawer and ran to the door, surprised but eager. I unlocked the door and let him in.

Travis wiped his damp forehead with the back of one arm. "That fog is awful," he said.

"How did you drive in it?" I asked him.

"I didn't." He pulled off a windbreaker and dropped it over the back of a chair. "Actually, I don't live too far from here, so I walked." He looked around. "Where's your mom?"

"In Austin. She flew there this morning, but couldn't get back because of the fog." I couldn't help it. I let out another sigh of relief. "I'm awfully glad you're here, Travis."

He put his hands on my shoulders and studied my face. "You were scared, weren't you?"

"A little. You know the things that have happened, and I keep thinking about what you said about someone wanting us out of here and maybe coming back for something he'd left."

"I was just guessing, trying to answer your questions. I'm sorry now I said anything. I didn't mean to scare you, Katie."

"I was reading when I realized that the dogs were barking, so I knew someone was coming, and then I heard footsteps on the walk and—"

His lips felt so intense, my knees wobbled as I returned his kiss.

Finally, he pulled back and looked into my eyes. "I'll stay as long as you want me to, Katie. I'll stay all night, if that's what you want."

"No," I said, too loudly, too quickly. Trying to breathe normally I told Travis, "Since Mom's not here, you really shouldn't be here either. She's got strict rules."

"Even when she's not here?"

"Especially when she's not here. I have rules too."

He smiled. "I came to see you in all this fog, and you're going to throw me out without even offering me something to eat?"

"There are no rules regarding the kitchen," I said, returning his smile. "What would you like? We've got a fudge pie in the freezer and a few oatmeal cookies left, or I could make you a ham sandwich. You name it."

We poked through the refrigerator, then agreed on the fudge pie, which was frozen so solid we had to hack our way into it.

When we'd finished demolishing our slices, laughing and wiping fudge smears from each other's face, Travis took my hand and said, "Don't you think you can trust me enough to tell me?"

"Tell you what?"

"Where Lana Jean's journal is."

I wasn't sure why his obsession with her journal bothered me so much. Even so, my first impulse was to hand it over to him—all those embarrassing, detailed pages. I realized he might destroy it, but the fact remained that it was still Lana Jean's property, which she'd entrusted to me. If I told him this, I'd be in for an argument I probably wouldn't win, so I tried to look blank. "Isn't the journal at her house?"

"It is not there," he said. "I went to see, and even helped her mom look for it." He paused and his eyes were so dark and serious I couldn't read them. "I think Lana Jane gave those pages to you."

I didn't want to out-and-out lie to Travis. What could I say?

At that moment the dogs set up another frantic warning, and I heard a car stop in front of our house.

"Someone's coming," I said. The heavy tread of footsteps echoed along the walkway.

"I see what you mean about the dogs being your warning system." As Travis got up and strode to the door, throwing it open, I followed.

Sheriff Granger paused only to give Travis a questioning look as he stomped into the kitchen, shaking beads of water from his jacket and cap. "Your mama called me," he told me. "She told me you were supposed to go to a friend's, but then was afraid the fog was too thick for you to get there. This is not the friend she mentioned."

As he glanced from me to Travis, I said, "Travis came by a few minutes ago, doing just what you're doing, making sure I was all right. I'd appreciate it if you'd give him a lift home. He walked here."

"Okay by me," he said, "but I have somethin' to say before I go. I didn't tell your mama because I didn't want to add to her worries. Just afore the fog set in, Lana Jean Willis's body was found out in the woods."

"Her body?" I whispered.

"Yeah. Boyd Morris's old hound got to nosin' around a clearing near the highway and next thing Boyd knew was he saw a hand stickin' up through the leaves. Shook him up pretty bad, but he came and got me."

I wasn't sure if I'd closed my eyes or if the room had suddenly grown dark. I tried taking deep breaths, but my lungs couldn't seem to handle them.

Travis rested a firm hand on my shoulder, but his voice quavered as he asked the sheriff, "Are you sure who it was?"

"Real sure. Mrs. Willis already identified the body."

"How was she killed?" Travis asked.

"Strangled. We'll need the county medical examiner to confirm, but he's pretty certain from the bruises on her neck."

I sat on the nearest chair, dropping my head between my knees, and it helped. The buzzing and flickering lights dissolved, and I could think clearly again.

"Are you okay, Katie?" Travis asked. "You aren't going to faint or anything?"

"I'm all right," I said, and gratefully leaned against him.

"I notified the Houston police," the sheriff told us. "That murderer-rapist they're lookin' for—it had to be him."

"For a minute I forgot," I said bitterly. "You don't have any crimes in Kluney." My anger growing, I said, "Lana Jean shouldn't have been killed! She shouldn't! Why do you blame everyone outside of Kluney for crimes that happen inside Kluney?"

His face reddened. "What crimes we get usually come from outside."

"Of course," I snapped, and counted them on my fingers. "One, shoplifting; two, burglaries; three—"

"Katie! Stop it!" Travis said. He gave me an odd look, then turned to the sheriff and began to apologize for me. "She's in shock. She didn't mean what she said."

I wanted to shout, "I did too!" but I realized that Mom would have done just what Travis was doing, and I said, "I'm sorry. I shouldn't have been rude."

Sheriff Granger walked to the door and held it open for Travis. "If you need anythin', you've got the number of the station. Just give a call. They'll get me on the radio."

Radio . . . another unanswered question. "Could I ask you a question, Sheriff Granger? That radio we found here at our house . . . Did you ever discover who it belonged to?"

"Miz Jocie Baker," he said. "But don't go suspectin' her of breakin' into your house. Eighty years old and wouldn't hurt a fly. That radio was on the list of things that got stolen when her house was burglarized last month."

"Do you have any idea how it got into *our* house?"

"No," he said, "and it's the least of my worries right now."

"Katie shouldn't be alone—" Travis began, but I firmly shook my head.

"I am fine. Honest." I wasn't pretending. I needed to be alone, because I had an awful lot to think about. "I'll call my mother at her hotel. She'll appreciate that both of you came to check on me. Thanks. Good night."

CHAPTER FOURTEEN

As I sat alone on the couch, I started to think. Whoever had burglarized Mrs. Baker's house, and was interrupted burglarizing ours, hadn't been leaving us any gifts or souvenirs. The radio had been here, and he was taking it away. Had he stashed the things he'd stolen in this old house, thinking that no one would bother to search it? Was he the one who had tried to scare us away, and when we hadn't left, had come back to collect his loot? Was our burglary just a cover-up?

At first it made sense, but then it began to get fuzzy. Mom and I had cleaned every inch of the house from top to bottom. If anything had been hidden away, we would have found it.

From top to bottom?

I walked into the hallway and glanced up at the rectangular door fitted into the ceiling. Then I remembered that when we were getting this house ready to live in I'd asked Mom if we should clean the attic, and she said there was no need to clean up there.

I reached up and tugged at the short length of rope that hung from the rectangle and pulled down the folding stairs that led up into the attic. Was there a light switch up there? I had no idea. I got a flashlight, tried not to think about mice and cockroaches, and carefully climbed the stairs.

The moment my head poked above the attic floor I swept my light around in every direction. Ugh! I'd been right about mouse droppings. The attic, which stank from dust and mildew, was filthy.

I sneezed, raising a cloud of dust, and quickly climbed up the rest of the stairs. There were footprints . . . lots of footprints. Mom's uncle Jim hadn't made these footprints, because they were far too new. And so was the small television set at one side of the small space and the microwave next to it. Just as I'd suspected, this is where the thief had stashed the things he'd stolen. Mom and I had interrupted him before he'd been able to get them all out of our house.

But who was the thief? In this perfect town of Sheriff Granger's Kluney, who could he be—and was there more than one? Could they be the beach bums who'd been seen around here?

At the sound of a faint rustling in the corner, I quickly left the attic and raised the stairs into place, making sure the door was snug.

With Mom away, I had no desire to call the sheriff and

show him what I'd found. I wasn't sure it would do any good, aside from a couple of people getting their stolen property back, and they could wait. They didn't need it tonight.

I made a mug of hot tea, with lots of lemon juice and honey and cinnamon in it—comfort tea, as Mom calls it—and curled back up on the sofa to sip it.

One, two, three kept coming back to my mind. *One, two, three. One* . . . shoplifting; *two* . . . petty burglaries; *three* . . . major thefts; *four* . . . If there was a pattern to the crimes in Kluney, each group of crimes getting more severe, then drifters or beach bums couldn't be responsible. The criminals had to be local—someone on hand to make the pattern work.

The answer came so suddenly I jumped, sloshing tea down my shirt and onto my jeans.

I snatched Lana Jean's journal pages out from under the sofa cushion and began reading, more carefully than I'd ever read anything before.

Travis, Travis, and more about Travis. I came to a mention of B.J. checking out Mrs. Walgren's set of four black hoods for a skit in drama. "Very funny," Lana Jean wrote, "because B.J. hadn't signed up for drama, and neither had his friends."

Lana Jean went on to describe what Travis ate for lunch. I lay the pages on my lap and concentrated on what I'd read. Black hoods. Black cloth? Could the scrap of black cloth I'd found have come from one of the hoods?

What had she written earlier? "One, two, three, four,

171

five, getting harder all the time, and if you don't, you're out."

Four . . . The crimes were getting more difficult and more daring. Could *four* have been a planned armed robbery? And could that armed robbery have gone wrong and turned into murder?

"The guys in Blitz have to prove themselves," Lana Jean had said.

With Lana Jean dead it was up to me to do some proving. I owed her that.

In agony I closed my eyes, but I could see Travis's face, his smile, his dark eyes . . . I could feel his kiss.

"No," I groaned, and dove into the journal pages again, concentrating on what I was reading to keep from dwelling on my own feelings about Travis. I read Lana Jean's entire entry about the carnival: how Travis and his friends had gone on some of the rides, what they had eaten, which carny games they'd played, even a jealous mention of the cheerleader Travis had met behind the Ferris wheel. And, finally, I read that one by one Travis and his friends had slipped away into the woods to find . . . a pigeon?

I was stumped. It actually took me a few minutes before I realized that Lana Jean had taken literally what she'd overheard. Now I knew better. I could see Travis and the others following the tracks of a carnival worker who had probably been looking for a quick and private place to goof off from his job. Their pigeon.

Travis, the leader of his friends in Blitz . . . Had he robbed the worker at gunpoint, then pulled the trigger?

Lana Jean hadn't been simply a victim of wishful thinking. She'd been telling the truth about Travis asking to take her out. Travis had been the one who had lied. Filled with an aching, cold misery, I realized that when Travis discovered that Lana Jean must have seen or overheard enough to place the members of Blitz with the carnival worker, he must have killed her. I was grief stricken. Pathetic Lana Jean dead and Travis a killer.

But who would believe me? How could I possibly prove it?

My head throbbed as I tried to put everything together. I must have fallen asleep on the sofa because I woke the next morning to see that the sun was rapidly burning away the fog. I stacked Lana Jean's journal pages. I had to hide this important evidence. Now I knew why Travis was so eager to get his hands on these pages—he wasn't embarrassed—he was protecting himself. I folded them and decided a safe place was to stuff them inside the outside packaging for a frozen carton of chicken à la king, and put it underneath an assortment of frozen stuff in the freezer compartment of the refrigerator. If Travis came searching for the pages, I doubted he'd think of looking there.

In order to dispose of the frozen chicken à la king, I stuck it into the oven and ate it for breakfast.

Mom would be home soon. I hadn't called her because I didn't want her to be worried. After giving the situation plenty of thought, I finally decided to keep everything to myself for just a little while. Mom would naturally call the sheriff, and all my suspicions would be out in the open, with no one able to prove things one way or another.

There'd be even more reason for people to want us out of here, and Mom would never get her novel written.

I had an idea, and I was counting on B.J.'s mean disposition to help me follow through.

When Mom got home, she was so busy, it was easy to tell her that she could see I was still in one piece, and avoid any other questions. Two inspectors came with her from Austin, and they all headed for the Hawkins Brothers Waste Disposal company. Mom asked if I'd like to go with them, but I knew they didn't need me, and I had other things to work on.

"Can't," I said. "I've got a lot of homework to do, and first, I've got to make a trip to the library to check out a copy of *The Three Musketeers.*"

"You read that last year," Mom said. "Is your class repeating it?"

"No," I said. "This is for an interpretation." In answer to the question in her eyes I said, "Interpretations are complicated. I'll explain later."

Mom gave me a lift to the library, and after I'd checked out the book I walked home, talking to each of the dogs who guarded the road to our house. They barked at me anyway. That was their job, and I was glad they were good at it.

I worked the rest of the afternoon, interrupted by a few angry, anonymous telephone calls and people who just called and hung up. Word about the Hawkins brothers company was getting around town fast.

Late that evening at dinner, Mom explained to me what a great day she'd had. "There exists a Resource Conservation and Recovery Act," she said. "Violators must pay fines." Then she went on about a superfund of federal money that could be used to clean up certain waste dump sites, with the companies responsible for the dumping having to pay back the money. When Bubba and Billy Joe Hawkins were faced with the inspectors, they'd named other violators, so a massive inspection and clean-up was going to take place in this part of Texas.

"The Hawkinses won't go out of business," Mom said. "They'll just have to change the way they do things."

"Some people called here. They didn't give their names, but they were pretty steamed about what you were doing."

"They just don't understand the dangers of toxic waste," Mom said, looking kind of sad. "All some people think about is making money, no matter what, and they don't want to face any problems that might threaten the loss of their jobs."

"What will happen to Anita Boggs and her little boy?"

"She finally gave permission for soil testing, as did the other three homeowners on that block. The Hawkinses may relocate them to new homes, or there may be lawsuits that take care of the problem, but, believe me, it's going to be taken care of, as it should be."

She put down her fork and smiled at me. "Enough about the Hawkins brothers. You are a great daughter. I hated to leave you alone, and I hope you don't mind that I had the sheriff check on you. The fog was so bad. . . ."

I didn't have to answer. We got three angry phone calls in a row. Mom tried to explain, then gave up because the callers didn't want explanations, and neither did the others who continued to call. Mom finally took the phone off the hook so we could go to bed.

On Sunday, after church, Mom and I went to call on Mrs. Willis to offer our sympathy and support. I knew how it felt to lose someone you love. So did Mom. We had the loss of my father only six years ago. But next to that, facing Mrs. Willis was the hardest thing I've ever had to do.

CHAPTER FIFTEEN

The next morning, just before Mrs. Walgren called the class to order, I searched her prop closet. There was no sign of the four black hoods, so I told her I needed them for my interpretation and asked if someone had checked them out.

She looked through a little spiral notebook and called, "B.J.—those black hoods you borrowed for your drama assignment . . . Is the assignment over? Can you bring the hoods back to class? Katie wants to use them for her interpretation."

He mumbled something, and I said, "I need them tomorrow."

"For practice?" Mrs. Walgren asked.

I'd rehearsed what I was planning to say, and I let it all spill out. "I know you gave us two weeks to work on our interpretations, but mine is ready, and I hope you'll let me put it on tomorrow."

Mrs. Walgren's look of surprise quickly disappeared and she clasped her hands together. "I'm counting on you for a top-notch interpretation," she said. "You know, it might be a fine idea for you to give yours first. It may inspire a few others in the class."

"Thank you," I said.

"Suppose you choose the students who will help you enact your interpretation," she said, and added a little dubiously, "I hope you'll have enough time to rehearse."

I said the first thing that came into my head. "The success of my interpretation is based on spontaneity."

It must have sounded good, because she smiled and said, "My goodness! This will be something different. I can hardly wait to see it."

As I walked back to my seat, B.J. glared and stuck out a foot to trip me, but I'd been expecting something. I stepped over his foot and sat down.

Wait until tomorrow, I thought as I stared at the back of B.J.'s head. *Tomorrow, when you find out what I'm going to do to you, you'll be in for a big surprise.*

Everyone at school was discussing Lana Jean's murder. I knew there was no way in the world I'd be able to talk to Travis and disguise what I'd learned, so I went to the nurse's office during lunch, told her I had an upset stomach —which I would have had if I'd met up with Travis—and spent the time lying on a cot. I recovered when the bells rang for my next class, and after school I went out a side door and cut behind the lineup of cars to get on the school bus in order to avoid him.

On the ride home, Tammy asked me questions about Lana Jean's murder, which I couldn't handle and told her so.

"I understand. You were her only real friend," Tammy said, and she changed the subject to how much fun she'd had visiting her aunt.

A real friend? When I'd been only too eager to drop Lana Jean and spend my time with Tammy and Julie and anyone else who showed even a scrap of friendliness. When I kissed Travis, *who'd—*

"Did you just groan?" Tammy asked. "Is something the matter?"

"I'm okay," I said, but I wasn't.

I didn't sleep much Monday night. I tried hard not to think about Lana Jean, and went over and over in my mind what I was going to say and do the next morning in English lit. It was either the worst idea I'd ever had or the best, and I wouldn't know until I tried it out.

What if B.J. wouldn't cooperate? What if he didn't bring the black hoods? What if he brought three of them, but not the one that was torn? What if I had guessed wrong, and the hoods hadn't been worn by the members of Blitz? My bedclothes were tangled when I woke up in the morning, and I couldn't eat a bite of breakfast.

"You're coming down with something," Mom said. "Are you running a fever?"

I shook my head. "It's the interpretation for English lit.

I've never done one before, and it counts a lot toward our final grade."

I could shoot my grade down too, I realized, but at the moment that was the least of my worries.

As I entered Mrs. Walgren's classroom that morning, I spotted the hoods wadded on the edge of her desk. With trembling fingers I picked them up, carried them to her props closet, and examined them. All four hoods were there, and one of them—at the back—was missing the piece I'd found in the woods and had stuffed into my pocket before leaving home that morning. I shoved the other three into the closet, folded the torn hood so the hole didn't show, and got into my seat. My legs were so shaky they could hardly hold me up, and no matter how hard I tried to breathe normally, my breath kept coming in thin little gasps.

The minute the announcements were over and the intercom had squawked to a logical end, Mrs. Walgren took roll call, brought the class to order, and, with a wiggle, settled into her chair. She informed the class that I would be the first to present my literary interpretation. She called me to come up to the front of the room.

I picked up the black hood and slowly walked to the front. "I need B.J. to help me out," I told Mrs. Walgren.

"B.J., did you hear that?" Mrs. Walgren asked.

"I'll help you." Billy Don eagerly waved his hand.

"Thanks," I said, and gave Billy Don a smile. "But it's a special kind of part. It has to be B.J."

"No way," B.J. muttered, and slid farther down in his seat.

"I expect complete cooperation," Mrs. Walgren stated in a no-nonsense tone. When he didn't budge, she said, "Are you interested in repeating this class next semester?"

Grumbling under his breath, B.J. reluctantly shuffled up the aisle.

I slid a straight-backed visitor's chair from its usual place in the corner, and asked, "Will you sit here, please?"

As B.J. did, I stepped behind him, raised my voice, and said, "We are hereby gathered to bring charges against His Majesty's unworthy subject, d'Artagnan, who will henceforth be hooded." I slapped the hood over B.J.'s head before he knew what had happened to him.

"Hey! What's . . . ?" He reached up to pull off the hood.

But the sharpness in Mrs. Walgren's voice brought him to a halt. "Keep your hands in your lap, B.J.! This is an intriguing beginning, and you are not to spoil it. Do you understand?"

B.J. muttered something under his breath and slumped in his chair. His eyes glittered through the peepholes in the hood, glaring at me with anger.

"Thank you, your Honor," I said to Mrs. Walgren, and stepped around to the side of the chair.

"D'Artagnan," I began. "In association with your seniors, known as Athos, Porthos, and Aramis, you have formed an illegal association, dedicated to crime. Is that not correct?"

"No," B.J. muttered.

Somebody whispered loudly enough for me to hear, "I saw the movie. The Three Musketeers weren't criminals."

Ignoring her, I continued, "The four of you have long been criminals, and the derring-do is all for show. Whether you're known as swordsmen, adventurers, or Blitz, behind your fine words are the blackest of hearts."

B.J. started at the word *Blitz,* and sat upright.

"D'Artagnan, you're the one who was a tagalong, who fought so hard to get into the group. They didn't want you, did they, until you insisted you could be part of their misadventures?"

"Why'd you say *Blitz*? What are you talking about?" B.J. demanded.

"I'm talking about theft, to begin with," I answered. "Shall we go over the list? First, small things taken from stores, then larger items; next, burglaries of homes. One, two, three, four, five . . . getting harder all the time, and if you don't participate, you're out!"

"Where'd you hear that? This is supposed to be about the Three Musketeers, isn't it?"

"One is for shoplifting; *two,* petty theft; *three,* household burglary; *four,* armed robbery—"

"Cut it out!"

"But it went wrong. Who pulled the trigger, d'Artagnan? You know, and you can tell us. Why be loyal to them? They wouldn't be loyal to you. They didn't want you in their club in the first place."

"That's not true! It was my . . ."

He broke off, and I pounced. "D'Artagnan, the tagalong. Save yourself. Tell the truth."

B.J. squirmed in his chair. I could see that he was furious, and I hoped he was scared, too—scared enough to snitch. "Tell us, was it Athos who shot the worker? Porthos? Aramis? Or was it you? Someone's going to tell! Someone's going to pay for the crime of murder!"

B.J. jerked off the hood and jumped to his feet. His face was pale, and a muscle twitched near his mouth. "You're crazy!" he shouted.

I snatched the hood from his hand and held up the piece that had been torn away by the thorn bush. "Am I?" I asked. "Which one of you was wearing this hood and backed into a thorn bush? Was it when the worker refused to give you his money? Did he put up a fight? It was murder, d'Artagnan! And you know what happens to murderers!"

With a yell of rage, B.J. shoved over the chair and ran out of the room.

I picked up the chair, not sure exactly what to do. I remembered that all performers take bows, so I bowed formally to Mrs. Walgren and to the class and said, "Those who may think of themselves as heroes, able to commit any crime without hesitation because of their standing at court, might be nothing more than criminals to the community at large. I rest my case."

Mrs. Walgren's expression was a combination of bewilderment and pleasure. "Your presentation had some puzzling aspects, Katie, but it was very interesting. Quite an unusual viewpoint to think about. Tell B.J. to return, and we'll begin our discussion."

I opened the door and looked out, but the hall was empty. "He may not come back," I said. "He got kind of emotional."

"I didn't know he was such a good actor," Mrs. Walgren said.

"I didn't either." I folded the torn hood with its missing piece and pocketed it. "There were a couple of things I hoped he'd say—I mean, a couple of lines he left out that would have given some answers."

"Perhaps the class can come up with the answers," Mrs. Walgren said.

Julie raised her hand. "I don't think there *are* any answers. There are two sides to almost everything. Even in war, both sides think they're right and the other one is wrong."

"A good observation," Mrs. Walgren said. "But these men, as the prosecutor pointed out, are guilty of theft and even murder. Could those crimes ever be considered right?"

"They were in the movie," someone said. "My father has the video of the real ancient *Three Musketeers* with Gene Kelly in it."

"Forget the movie," Mrs. Walgren said. "We're using the novel as a base for our thinking. Are the actions taken by the Three Musketeers and d'Artagnan considered crimes, punishable by law, as our prosecutor would have us believe?"

A boy near the window waved his hand, and Mrs. Walgren said, "Yes, Arthur?"

"Could I sharpen my pencil?" he asked.

Fortunately, Julie spoke up. "If you put those four characters into today's world, they would be arrested and convicted. Even though they were protecting the queen, their country wasn't officially at war, so whatever their reason for murder, it's still murder."

The discussion went on, and I only half listened. I had learned one thing from B.J.'s fury and fear. I'd been right.

But B.J. had run off, and I had no idea where he'd gone. Was it to warn Travis and the others?

I was beginning to get a little scared myself, not knowing what B.J. was going to do. Maybe I was trying to take the law into my own hands, and maybe that wasn't such a good idea, after all.

CHAPTER SIXTEEN

I would have guessed that B.J. had warned the others in Blitz, but Duke and Delmar showed up for history as though nothing out of the ordinary had happened, and I gave a huge sigh of relief. Had I succeeded in making B.J. mad at them? And was he angry enough that he might decide to tell what he knew?

I spent lunchtime in the school library, and again, after classes were over, ducked out the side door to avoid Travis.

Now was the time to talk to Mom. I knew the sheriff wouldn't listen to me, but he'd have to listen to Mom— and soon. I nearly panicked when I got home and found a note telling me she'd driven Anita Boggs and her little boy to the Houston medical center.

"Don't expect me for dinner, honey," Mom had written. "But I should make it home no later than ten or eleven."

Not today, Mom, I silently begged. *Today I need you to be here.*

The dogs' barking alerted me to the car that had pulled up in front of our house. I made sure the door was securely locked before I looked out the window and saw the sheriff thudding his way up our walk.

I fumbled with the locks, then threw open the door. "I was going to call you," I told him.

"We need to talk," he said. "You, me, and your mama."

"Mom's not here," I explained as I followed him into the living room. "She went to Houston, but she'll be back soon."

He sat down and motioned to me to take a seat. "Then I'll keep this short. First place, you shoulda told me what you knew and how you found out about it, instead of pullin' that silly dramatic scene in Mrs. Walgren's class."

"How did you know about that?" I asked.

"Mrs. Walgren's sharp. She started thinkin' about the things you told B.J. and right away remembered the carnival worker, so she called me. Where'd you get this information?"

"From Lana Jean's journal. She was crazy about Travis, so she wrote about nearly everything he did. She wrote about the four members of Blitz going into the woods after a pigeon. She took them literally. She didn't understand what they were talking about."

I filled him in on the reason for Blitz and what Travis, B.J., Duke, and Delmar had been doing. I gave Sheriff Granger the hood and the torn piece that fit it. Then I pulled the chicken à la king box out of the freezer and handed him the sheets torn out of Lana Jean's journal. "Everything I told you is written on these pages," I said.

He slowly shook his head. "I've known these boys and their families for more years than I'd care to count." He looked up at me. "Do you know which one of 'em killed the carnival worker?"

"No," I said, "but I think—"

The phone rang, interrupting me, and Sheriff Granger answered it, as though it was his house, not ours. He lowered his voice as he talked to someone, so I guessed he'd been expecting the call, and when he hung up he frowned at me. "Maybe you can tell me this—where'd the boys go off to?"

"They're gone?"

"They sure are. I sent a deputy to pick them up—just for questioning—but not one of 'em can be found." He stomped to the door, adding as an afterthought, "If you come up with anything else, call the dispatcher. I've got a new man on, but he'll get in touch with me, and I'll be right out."

"Thanks," I said, and made sure the door was securely locked as soon as the sheriff had left. Even though the long afternoon shadows hadn't yet melted into a purple twilight, I went throughout the house, turning on every light, inside and out. The knowledge that no one knew where Travis, Duke, Delmar, and B.J. were made me very uncomfortable. No—a lot more than uncomfortable. I was scared right down to my toenails.

There was no way I was going to stay here by myself. As I picked up the phone my fingers trembled so violently I nearly dropped the receiver. When Tammy answered, relief flooded through my body like warm tea and for a moment I had trouble talking.

"Is that you, Katie?" Tammy asked. "Is something wrong?"

"Yes," I said. "Could I come over to your house?"

"Sure," she said. "Come right now."

I suddenly remembered I didn't have transportation, and there was no way I was going to walk the distance to Tammy's house in the dark. I told her.

"Darn," she said. "Mom just drove to the grocery store, and Dad took the pickup into town to a board meeting of the Rotary Club. Is it okay if Mom or I come by for you after she gets home? It should be only around an hour."

"That's okay. See you then," I said, and hung up. I suppose I should have called the dispatcher or someone, but I just sat on the sofa, feet together, hands in my lap, and waited.

I wasn't sure who or what I was waiting for. Tammy? Mom? Travis?

Forty-five long minutes later, when it was close to eight o'clock and as dark as it could possibly get, I heard the dogs bark. As usual, it began with the Lab, baying a warning to whoever dared to pass the fence that stood between them. The German shepherd picked up the warning, and soon the rottweiler added his snarls and deep-throated barks.

My hands were so clammy they could hardly hold the phone, but I managed to dial the number of the sheriff's office. "I think someone's on our road," I babbled at the dispatcher. "The neighbors' dogs are barking, which means someone's coming, and—"

"Okay, lady," he said in a hurried voice. "I'll make a note of it."

"My name is Katherine Gillian," I told him, "and I live at—" I realized that he'd hung up and I was talking to myself.

With the outside lights on, at least I could see if someone came into our yard. I sneaked back the drapes to peer outside, but let them fall when I heard the shot.

I dropped to the floor and lay there, with my arms over my head, until I realized that the shot hadn't been meant for me. Two of the dogs continued their frantic barking, but the Lab was still.

"No!" I whispered, so horrified I couldn't move. "He wouldn't shoot the dogs!" But I heard another shot, and the German shepherd was abruptly silent.

I froze, too numb to move or think until the third shot came and I heard someone running toward our house.

Terrified, I stumbled to the phone, jabbing at the buttons long after I realized there was no dial tone. He'd cut the telephone line.

Suddenly the lights went out, and I cried out in fear. He had access to the breaker box, and he had a gun. Soon he'd smash his way into our house, and I'd have no way of protecting myself!

Oh, Travis! For a while you made me believe you! How could I have been so stupid?

I scrambled along the floor, mindlessly searching for a place to hide, until my mind cleared and I realized I

191

couldn't hide. Not in this little house, which he knew so well. Hadn't Travis told me I should be glad we had such a small house to clean, with only four rooms and a bath? I'd heard him say it, yet I'd been so befuddled with Travis himself, I hadn't realized at the time what his words meant.

The answer to the only possible way of protecting myself came as I heard a fumbling at the kitchen door. The attic! I'd hide in the attic! Bouncing off the walls in my haste, I ran into the hall and groped until I felt the rope. I tugged at it, pulled down the attic door, and stumbled up the steps. The moment I reached the attic floor I pulled the stairs up behind me.

How I wished I had a flashlight! Behind me were little scuttling sounds, but below me was the crash of broken window glass, and I was caught in the middle.

I could hear one pair of footsteps, and doors opening and shutting, as the murderer searched for me. He knew I was somewhere in the house. I wished I'd had the presence of mind to open the door to the porch so he might think I'd run down the beach, but it was too late for wishes. It was just a matter of time until he pulled down the stairs to the attic.

I heard him walk into the hallway and stop directly below the stairs. As he chuckled gleefully, I froze. Terrified, startled into a new and sharp awareness, I began to remember things I had heard and seen and tucked away, unheeded. In my mind I could clearly visualize the murderer, his eyes glinting as he smiled. Any moment now, he'd be coming after me.

I did the only thing possible. Heedless of the noise I

made, I picked up the portable television set, shivering so violently it nearly fell out of my arms.

The door, with its attached stairs, slid downward slowly, a flickering light around the opening showing me he had a flashlight—maybe my own flashlight. There was a soft thump as the stairs dropped into place, and shadows stretched upward like giant fingers reaching to peel me out of my hiding place.

He chuckled again and whispered, "I know you're up there, Katie, and I'm coming to get you."

I didn't wait until he reached the attic. The moment he began to climb the stairs I did the only thing left for me to do. I dropped the television set on his head.

CHAPTER SEVENTEEN

The dispatcher may have thought I was some nervous nut, scared of the dark, but when he laughingly told the sheriff about someone calling because dogs were barking on her road, the sheriff knew what to do. At least, that's what he told me after he'd called an ambulance to take B.J. to the hospital.

"Check the television set and the microwave in the attic for fingerprints," I told him. "And B.J.'s gun too. Ballistics will match his gun with the bullet that killed the carnival worker."

"You through tellin' me how to do my job?" he asked, then seemed to relent as he added, "We got us a good case. Travis turned up with Duke and Delmar, all of 'em scared puppies, yippin' out everythin' they know about B.J. gettin' 'em into all this. According to what they told me, the

195

robbery got out of hand, and B.J. panicked, pullin' the trigger. Far as Lana Jean's concerned, the others didn't know what B.J. had done until afterward."

"They're just as guilty as he is," I said.

"Maybe, if you're talkin' about being morally wrong," he said, "but turnin' state's evidence, they won't get near the same sentence as B.J." He paused and thought a moment. "B.J.'s family came to Kluney around the late fifties, from New Jersey, as I remember."

I couldn't keep the sarcasm out of my voice. "So that makes them outsiders," I said. "But B.J. was born in Kluney."

Sheriff Granger threw me a suspicious look, but he said, "When young people choose evil over good it's a terrible waste. Edmund Burke wrote, 'What shadows we are, and what shadows we pursue.'"

And what shadows we create, I thought. *B.J.—so desperate to feel important that he'd conceived the idea of Blitz, and so furious at being mislabeled a tagalong in class, instead of the instigator of the crimes, that he'd almost given it away by saying, "It was my . . ." My idea.*

The sheriff said he'd stay with me until my mama came home, but I wasn't frightened any longer, just terribly, terribly angry that because four guys had been so stupid two innocent people had been killed.

In spite of all that had happened, I went to the Future Farmers dance with Billy Don. I actually had a good time. It felt good to be doing some normal high school stuff. I told Billy Don I'd be leaving Kluney, and yet, I felt happy to have a good memory of the place, because the dance was fun.

During August, Mom finished her novel, and we moved back to Houston. I returned to the High School for the Performing Arts and my wonderful ballet instructor.

Finally, I was honest with Mom. "The way your love of writing gets inside you and you can't think of anything else —that's how my dancing makes me feel."

"You never told me," Mom said.

"If I had, you wouldn't have moved to Kluney and written your novel." I grinned and asked, "Aren't you glad now I didn't?"

At first I was happy to be home, relieved to be far away from the shadowmakers and all the fear and pain they'd caused. But almost immediately Mom became involved in investigating a huge housing development that had been built in northeast Houston on landfill that covered a toxic waste dump, and last weekend eight people in Houston were killed in drive-by shootings, fights, and robberies at gunpoint.

I realized there are shadowmakers of all kinds, and you can't hide from them. They're everywhere.

Can something be done about them?

Only if we try.

About the Author

JOAN LOWERY NIXON is the author of more than ninety books for young readers, including *A Candidate for Murder, Whispers from the Dead,* and *Secret, Silent Screams.* She has served as regional vice-president for the Southwest Chapter of the Mystery Writers of America, and is the only three-time winner of the Edgar Allan Poe Best Juvenile Mystery Award given by that society. She received the award for *The Kidnapping of Christina Lattimore, The Séance,* and *The Other Side of Dark,* which also was a winner of the California Young Reader Medal.

Joan Lowery Nixon lives in Houston with her husband.